What was Rafe thinking?

Her glance collided with his, but his expression remained shuttered.

It was some time later that Rafe pinned her with his dark gaze. He smiled twistedly as he came toward her carrying a glass of champagne. "Shall we drink to a profitable union?"

"You mean a profitable *purchase,* don't you?" Jo's mask of serenity slipped momentarily to reveal her repugnance. "You bought me, remember? The transaction has been signed and sealed. All that's left is for me to deliver. Not so, Rafe?"

His mouth thinned and a muscle twitched along the side of his square jaw. She'd angered him—she recognized the signs— but his overall expression remained as inscrutable as before.

"I stand corrected." His coldly dispassionate glance flicked over her. "I shall drink instead to my latest and most profitable acquisition."

YVONNE WHITTAL, a born dreamer, started scribbling stories at an early age but admits she's glad she didn't have to make her living by writing then. "Otherwise," she says, "I would surely have starved!" After her marriage and the birth of three daughters, she began submitting short stories to publishers. Now she derives great satisfaction from writing full-length books. The characters become part of Yvonne's life in the process, so much so that she almost hates coming to the end of each manuscript and having to say farewell to dear and trusted friends.

Books by Yvonne Whittal

HARLEQUIN PRESENTS

HARLEQUIN ROMANCE

Don't miss any of our special offers. Write to us at the following address for information on our newest releases.

Harlequin Reader Service
P.O. Box 1397, Buffalo, NY 14240
Canadian address: P.O. Box 603,
Fort Erie, Ont. L2A 5X3

YVONNE WHITTAL

valley of the devil

Harlequin Books

TORONTO • NEW YORK • LONDON
AMSTERDAM • PARIS • SYDNEY • HAMBURG
STOCKHOLM • ATHENS • TOKYO • MILAN

Harlequin Presents first edition February 1992
ISBN 0-373-11438-9

Original hardcover edition published in 1991
by Mills & Boon Limited

VALLEY OF THE DEVIL

CHAPTER ONE

'I THINK it's time you told her, Danny.'

'Told me what?' Joceline Harris was instantly on the alert with a growing uneasiness clutching at the pit of her stomach when she looked away from her mother to direct a sharp, questioning glance at her brother. 'What is it that I haven't been told?'

Danny looked back at her grimly, and he was about to say something when their mother intervened impatiently to lift the lid on the problem.

'We could lose everything, Jo! *Everything!* Our home, the business...' Lavinia's grey-green eyes mirrored the note of panic in her voice. 'Your father would turn in his grave if he knew!'

Joceline wondered if she looked as confused as she felt. Her mother had hinted at bankruptcy. Was it possible?

'If you don't mind, Mum,' Daniel Harris looked vaguely annoyed, 'I'd like to talk to Jo alone for a few minutes.'

Lavinia tilted her silvery head to look up at her son, who had risen from his chair to take up a familiar stance in front of the stone fireplace, and she sighed resignedly as she rose to leave; but she paused briefly at the living-room door to cast a quick, anxious glance at her daughter. 'Please, Jo. You've *got* to help us.'

Help? How could she possibly help? Jo wondered, waiting until she could hear her mother's footsteps echoing across the hall towards the stairs before she got up to join her brother in front of the fire. 'What's this all about, Danny?'

Her voice was warm and faintly husky. She had the natural ability to soothe and calm the most anxious patients in her hospital ward, but the soothing quality in her voice seemed to have no effect on the nervous agitation that gripped the fair-haired man who stood with his back to the glowing coals in the grate.

'Harris Construction is no longer the thriving company it used to be a couple of years ago,' he explained, frowning darkly into the glass of whisky he held in his hand. 'The economy in southern Africa has put a financial squeeze on the smaller companies.'

'Tell me something I don't know,' she prompted quietly, studying her brother closely for the first time that evening.

Danny was thirty, five years her senior, but he was under obvious stress that evening, and his greyish pallor seemed to add several uncomplimentary years to his age.

'Our home has been mortgaged to the hilt, the business has been running at a loss, and my credibility at the bank has reached down to a level where the bank manager has found it necessary to threaten me with the foreclosure of my existing loan.' Danny downed his whisky in one gulp and lit a cigarette with hands that shook. 'It sounds hopeless, but there is a way out of this financial mess,' he added, smoke jetting from his nostrils. 'I've just landed a contract that could pull us out of the red at the bank in a couple of years.'

'So what's the problem?'

'A shortage of liquid cash.' His eyes, grey-green like their mother's, were troubled and anxious. 'I'd be cutting my own throat if I delved into my capital to keep the bank happy. What I need is a private loan to pay the ten per cent guarantee on the contract, and if I don't want this opportunity to slip through my fingers I need to have the money within the next two weeks.'

Jo was beginning to feel the panic she had glimpsed in her mother's eyes. 'I can appreciate the urgency of the situation, Danny, but I fail to see how I can help you.'

'There's only one person I can think of who might be in a position to give us the financial assistance we need.' Danny held Jo's steady, questioning gaze for a moment, then he looked away and drew hard on his cigarette. 'He never had a very high opinion of *me*, but he might consider it if *you* asked him.'

Understanding sent a shiver of icy shock racing up Jo's spine and her green eyes widened in alarm. 'Not *Rafe*!' she exclaimed, her voice rising a pitch higher with agitation. 'You can't be serious, Danny. Not *Rafe*!'

Danny had the grace to look embarrassed, but there was desperation in his eyes. 'He's my last hope, Jo.'

'I couldn't ask Rafe. I just *couldn't* do that, Danny. Not after...' The words became strangled in Jo's throat, and she was visibly pale and shaken when she backed away from her brother to sit down heavily on the arm of the chair she had vacated earlier. 'What you're asking is impossible, Danny.' The flames in the grate were trapped in the rich auburn of her shoulder-length hair as she shook her head. 'There *has* to be some other way!'

'Dammit, Jo, there *is* no other way except to ask for a private loan!' Danny was equally pale as he took an urgent pace towards her, and she could see pearly beads of perspiration glistening on his forehead and upper lip. 'Can you think of anyone else who might be in a position to help us?' he demanded, his voice cracking with anxiety.

'No, but——'

'*Please*, Jo!' He flicked the butt of his cigarette into the fire and reached for her hands. His fingers were cold and clammy when they gripped hers, and she could feel the terrible tremors of anxiety that were coursing through his body. 'I can't throw away everything Dad worked so hard for, and Rafe will help us if you ask him. I *know* he will! Please, Jo, say you'll ask him. *Please!*'

Joceline Harris stood tall and straight at the window. It was a hazy June morning, and the shiver that raced through her could not be blamed entirely on the chill of winter in the air. She was watching the people going quickly about their business in a street lined with tall pear trees, but she was recalling the conversation she had had with Danny two days ago, and hearing again the urgent plea in his voice.

'Rafe will help us if you ask him. I *know* he will!'

Would he? Would Rafe help them?

She was not so sure, and a faintly strangled sound passed her lips as she turned away from the window to lower herself into a chair. She had tried desperately to think of an alternative solution, but she had failed, and that was why she was sitting in this partly deserted lounge of the Mirage Hotel in Beaufort West...waiting. Waiting for Rafe Andersen to join her.

Jo was outwardly calm and composed, and she had her rigorous training as a nurse to thank for that, but inwardly she was quaking with nerves. Rafe Andersen was the last person on this earth she would have wanted to turn to for help, but the situation was desperate, and her personal feelings were not important. Danny was making a daring bid to save their home and the construction company, and she dared not let him down.

Rafe's deep voice had been abrupt on the phone when she had called him at Satanslaagte to make this appointment. Three years had elapsed since the last time there had been any form of contact between them, and if he had been surprised to hear from her, then he had hidden it well. But Rafe had always been good at hiding his feelings, she remembered whimsically. Except when...!

Jo tugged sharply at the rein of her thoughts, but they sped on regardless of her urgent desire to forget the past. For three long years she had tried to banish from her mind the memory of her marriage to Rafe Andersen, but she had failed, just as she was failing now.

She had known Rafe a month when he had asked her to marry him. It had been long enough for Jo to realise that he was the man she wanted to spend the rest of her life with. She had wanted to take care of him and keep house for him on his sheep farm in the Karoo, but, sadly, her plans had gone awry. Rafe's mother had still been very much the mistress of the house, and Averil Andersen had made it clear to Jo that she had no intention of relinquishing that task.

Jo had approached the problem with understanding, knowing that it must be difficult for Averil to accept the fact that her son's wife had the right to make certain demands in the home, but Averil's armour against Jo had been impenetrable.

'You belong in the city, not here on a sheep farm,' Averil had said when Jo's fear of horses had made her decline Rafe's offer to teach her to ride.

And then there had been Lorin Scheepers.

Lorin was the beautiful blue-eyed, dark-haired daughter of a neighbouring farmer. She had been twenty-one at that time, the same age as Jo, and she had made no secret of the fact that she had nurtured the hope of marrying Rafe. She had resented Jo's presence at Satanslaagte, and she had used every conceivable excuse to invade what little time Jo could have had alone with Rafe, who had had to work almost day and night during those months to recoup his losses after the long, severe drought.

'You will never have the ability to give my son the happiness he deserves. He needs a wife like Lorin Scheepers who knows the land as well as he does,' Averil had announced one hot afternoon when they had watched Rafe and Lorin ride out on horseback across the semi-desert and into the shimmering summer heat.

Jo's growing despondency had robbed her of the desire to dispute her mother-in-law's theories. The truth had been undeniable. Lorin, like Rafe, had lived all her life on that semi-desert land, they had spoken the same language, and it was Jo who didn't belong.

The frustration and boredom of having nothing to do had finally taken its toll on Jo after long, agonising months of being treated like an outsider in her husband's home. Her dissatisfaction had led to petty arguments erupting between Rafe and herself, arguments which had always ended in Rafe accusing her of not making an effort to settle down, and Jo's inability to defend herself had filled her with a smouldering resentment. The truth would have raised the level of friction in the home, and that was the last thing Jo had wanted while she had still harboured the faint hope that her patience with Averil might eventually be rewarded.

That hope had faded swiftly when Jo finally realised that pressure of work on Rafe's side, and idleness on her own, had made them drift further and further apart until they no longer had anything to say to each other. The physical side of their marriage had become their only bond, but Jo had wanted more from marriage than that, and so, she believed, had Rafe.

It had been their inability to reach each other on any level other than the physical which had driven the final wedge between them, and Jo could still recall the look of obvious delight on Averil Andersen's face the day she had discovered that Rafe had moved out of the master bedroom.

'I knew you couldn't make my son happy.'

That 'I told you so' statement had had the effect of a heated rod entering a raw, aching wound. It had cauterised Jo's emotions, leaving her too numb to feel anything except oddly relieved when Rafe had confronted her that same day with the request for a divorce.

'Our marriage was a mistake,' he had said.

That was three years ago; three years of failing to understand how a marriage which had seemed so right could have gone so wrong.

Jo's thoughts shifted back to the present when a tray of tea was placed in front of her on the low circular table, and the muscles at the pit of her stomach contracted savagely as she signed the chit and handed it back to the waitress. Her appointment with Rafe was for ten o'clock, and it was almost that time now.

How do I look? Jo passed a shaky hand over her rich auburn hair coiled into a sensible knot at the nape of her neck and nervously fingered the heart-shaped silver pendant hanging on a chain about her throat. Have I changed much? Has Rafe?

A group of German tourists had gathered around a low table at the opposite end of the long lounge. They discussed their itinerary enthusiastically, but it was their laughter that captured Jo's attention briefly. Her glance shifted in their direction, and that was when she saw him.

Rafe!

He stood in the doorway, his tall, broad-shouldered frame almost blocking the entrance. He was a businessman of repute with an interest in computer and engineering companies across the country, but farming was in his blood, and even in his impeccably tailored cream trousers and brown suede jacket he still seemed to bear that indefinable stamp that classified him as a man of the earth. It had been that, rather than his rugged good looks, which had attracted Jo to Rafe in the first place, and she was dismayed to discover that the attraction was still just as powerful.

Dark eyes met hers across the room with a familiar stabbing precision that pinned her helplessly to her chair, and her heart was suddenly pounding in her throat, almost cutting off her air supply as Rafe crossed the carpeted length of the room with those firm, long-legged strides she remembered so well.

She panicked for an instant when he stood towering over her, but she regained control just as swiftly to extend her hand to him with a forced smile on her lips.

'Hello, Rafe.'

'Joceline.'

The cool, firm grip of his fingers on hers did not unnerve her as much as the abrupt usage of her full name, and then there was also that familiar hint of his favourite aftershave quivering in her nostrils.

'I hope you don't mind, but I took the liberty of ordering tea.' She slanted a quick, nervous glance at him as he lowered his long, muscular body into the chair close to hers. 'May I pour you a cup?'

Rafe nodded. 'I take it black and without sugar.'

'I remember.' There were so many things that Jo remembered; so many things she knew she would never forget. She forced her rigid facial muscles into a smile and prayed silently that Rafe wouldn't notice the slight tremor in her hand as she poured their tea and passed him a cup. 'How are things on the farm?'

'Why the sudden interest?'

Jo's breath caught in her throat when her attempt at civilised conversation was flung back at her. Rafe had always been a man of few words—it had been one of the many qualities she had admired in him—but now each word was a vicious barb, and it hurt.

'This is an extremely awkward situation for me, Rafe.' Jo thought she had prepared herself well for this meeting with the man who had once been her husband and her lover, but she had not foreseen the difficulties of having to face him like a stranger when everything about him was still so familiar. 'How is your mother?' she tried again.

'She's well.'

'Is she still living with you at Satanslaagte?'

'She is.' Rafe looked away briefly, giving Jo a glimpse of that tanned and familiar profile with the broad forehead, aquiline nose and square, determined jaw. 'My mother happens to be on a three-month visit to some of her relatives in England, and she's not due back for another two months.'

Jo hid her surprise behind a mask of indifference, but it was hard to imagine Averil Andersen leaving her earthy domain to indulge in something as daring as a lengthy visit to another country.

'I suppose you have Lorin to take care of you while your mother is away.' The words were out before Jo could censor her thoughts or put a leash on her tongue, and Rafe's dark, heavy eyebrows rose a fraction above eyes that flashed briefly with annoyance.

'I seldom see Lorin. She has a farm of her own to manage these days, and she doesn't have much time for anything else.'

An odd sense of relief washed over Jo. 'You haven't married her?'

The words were out again before she could stop them, and there was a gleam of derisive mockery in the narrowed eyes that drew hers like a magnet. 'What made you think I would?'

'You share so many similar interests,' she said with more caution this time.

She was not relaxed, but she wanted to give Rafe the impression that she was and, leaning back in her chair, she crossed one leg over the other, but she regretted the action.

The swish of her stockings drew Rafe's gaze to her booted foot before it lifted higher to follow the shape of her thigh beneath her blue tartan skirt, and the slow, intimate appraisal of those dark, hooded eyes made the blood drum faster through her veins.

Oh, no! It wasn't possible that he could still affect her in this way. *Damn* him!

'Why haven't *you* married again?' he asked, cutting into her angry, distracted thoughts, and it took a moment for Jo to gather her scattered wits about her.

'Once bitten, twice shy, I guess.' She squared her shoulders beneath her beige knitted sweater. 'I took back my maiden name after the divorce. The lawyer arranged it for me.'

Rafe accepted that statement in stony silence, but Jo felt like kicking herself. She could not imagine why she had considered it necessary to mention that fact. After three long years was there still enough bitterness left inside her to arouse a desire to hurt Rafe?

'I don't believe you drove all the way from Cape Town to Beaufort West to make polite conversation, Joceline, so let's get down to the reason why you wanted me to meet you here this morning.' Rafe brought matters sharply to a head when they had finished their tea, and Jo's hand shook visibly as she leaned forward in her chair to place her empty cup on the tray.

She had been mistaken in her belief that Rafe had not changed much since the last time she had seen him. There was a strange, savage quality about him that frightened her, and she felt sick inside at the thought of what she had to ask him.

'I was asked to—to approach you on behalf of my family,' she began haltingly, deciding to deliver the facts before she had to stoop to that distasteful level of begging, and she went on to explain the situation at home as Danny had related it to her.

Rafe listened to her plight without comment until her voice faded into silence, and Jo swallowed convulsively when she finally scraped together sufficient courage to meet his dark, steady gaze.

'If Danny loses this contract, then we lose everything my father worked so hard to preserve over the years,' she added, her voice lowered with the urgency of her appeal, and her insides racked by the same tremors she had felt in Danny two nights ago.

Rafe leaned back in his chair, his expression giving nothing away, and his response—when it finally came—blunt and emotionless. 'So it's money you want.'

'A loan,' she contradicted him distastefully, wincing inwardly and unaware that she was clasping and unclasping her hands in her lap with nervous anxiety. 'You're our last hope, Rafe,' she pleaded in desperation, 'and I swear I shall make it my personal responsibility to see that you're paid back every cent with interest.'

Rafe took his time to consider her request, and Jo felt the tension inside her rise to breaking-point as she watched him lace his fingers together across his chest and stretch his long legs out in front of him. To a stranger he might look relaxed, but there was a steely tautness in that muscled body that set Jo's nerves on edge, and she knew a sense of foreboding when those dark, smouldering eyes eventually met hers.

'How much do you need?'

'A hundred and fifty thousand.' She held her breath, waiting for Rafe's explosive reaction, but his rugged features remained immobile except for that ominous tightening of the muscles along the side of his jaw.

'I'll provide Danny with the financial assistance he needs if you'll agree to marry me again and provide me with an heir. I might reconsider the issue when you have fulfilled your part of the bargain and, if I'm in a generous mood, I might even allow Danny to look upon my financial assistance as an investment in the company rather than a loan.'

Jo had a curious sensation that the breath was being squeezed from her lungs, and she paled visibly. 'If this is intended as a joke, then it's in poor taste!'

'That's my offer, Joceline,' he said, shrugging his wide shoulders with a gesture of carelessness she had never known him to display before. 'Take it or leave it.'

She stared at his tanned, ruggedly handsome features, searching for some sign of softening, but his sensuous mouth had thinned to a harsh, uncompromising line that sent an icy shiver racing up her spine. 'What you're demanding is payment in blood! It's *immoral*!'

'It's the fairest deal I have to offer you,' Rafe countered with a flat finality that made the blood chill in her veins.

'You must be *mad*!'

'You may be right,' he agreed, watching her so intently that she was beginning to feel like a foreign specimen under microscopic examination.

'Why, Rafe?' she demanded, her voice lowered in a desperate attempt to remain calm. 'Why are you doing this?'

'Satanslaagte has been in the Andersen family for five generations, and I intend to keep it that way.'

'There is a more humane way of providing yourself with an heir for Satanslaagte. Why choose to do so in this loveless manner?' she reasoned with him, her throat so tight that it was an effort to speak. 'You're thirty-six, Rafe. You're still young enough to meet someone you could love, and you——'

'Love!' The word exploded disparagingly from his lips. 'Love is a grossly overrated emotion!'

His outburst did not surprise her. He had said 'I want you' often enough, but he had never said 'I love you'. Perhaps that was why he had found it so easy to say, 'It's over.'

'You might as well know that I'm not particularly interested in marriage, and most especially not now since I've had a taste of freedom again, so what I'm offering is a marriage with a difference.' Rafe smiled for the first time, but there was not even a fraction of warmth in those dark eyes that held Jo's captive. 'We both happen to be in need of something which the other can provide, and in this instance we can do so without having to pretend to something that isn't there.'

Pretend? Was that what Rafe believed she had been doing during those six months they had been married? Was that what *he* had done? Jo wondered about that while she fought back the wave of pain that threatened to engulf her.

'If I—if I agree,' she said, stammering as she felt herself losing that last fragile grip on her composure, 'what happens when I—I've provided you with an heir?'

Rafe was so still that he could have been carved in granite. Only his eyes moved, and they trailed over her body in a deliberate and insulting assessment before he answered her. 'You will naturally have the choice of staying or leaving. Either way will be immaterial to me, but the child will remain at Satanslaagte.'

The green of Jo's eyes was the only colour left in a face that had gone chalk-white, and her hands gripped the wooden arms of her chair for support as she felt herself start to shake with a rage she could not control. 'My God, you've become a cold-blooded, sadistic swine, and I——'

'I'd be a little more careful in my choice of words if I were you, Joceline,' he warned softly, a dangerous light flickering in his eyes as he leaned forward with an infuriating calmness to help himself to a second cup of tea. 'I might just change my mind and withdraw my offer completely.'

Jo pulled herself together with an effort. 'If I'm the beggar in this instance, then it's because circumstances demanded it, but I'm not enjoying it, Rafe Andersen. It's the most degrading task I've ever had to perform.'

'There wouldn't have been a need for you to place yourself in this degrading situation if Danny hadn't mismanaged the funds during those first couple of years after your father's death,' Rafe pointed out with a stabbing accuracy which Jo could not refute.

It was true. Danny had enjoyed life in the fast lane, and she now believed that he had foolishly squandered funds which could have prevented their present financial dilemma. The responsibility of taking charge of the Harris Construction company had changed her brother, but it was obvious that the change had come a little too late.

'Don't judge my brother too harshly,' she pleaded. 'Danny has changed, and he'll prove himself if you'll give him that chance.'

Rafe swallowed a mouthful of black tea and shrugged his wide shoulders once again with that unfamiliar display of unconcern. 'Whether Danny gets that chance or not depends entirely on you, Joceline.'

A lead weight settled in Jo's breast when she faced up to the facts. Rafe was not going to change his mind; she could see it in his challenging glance and in the relentless set of his jaw. The continued existence of her family home and business now depended solely on her decision. If she sold her body to Rafe, then he would give her family the financial assistance they so desperately needed, but if she refused...!

A burst of laughter from the group of tourists scraped across her raw nerves, and brought her perilously close to tears.

'I can't simply sit back and watch the destruction of something for which my father almost slaved himself to death. It would kill my mother, and... Oh, God!' she ended on a groan, raising a hand to press her thumb and third finger against her throbbing temples.

'I take it, then, that you agree to the conditions of the loan?'

She lowered her hand to her lap at the sound of that deep, gravelly voice and nodded bleakly. 'I have no choice.'

Rafe's expression didn't alter, it remained inscrutable as he drained his cup and placed it on the tray. 'Very well,' he said curtly. 'I'll drive down to Cape Town on Monday to make the necessary arrangements. I dare say you'll have a few arrangements of your own to make, and I suggest you don't drag it out. I want us to be married by the end of next week.'

Jo was caught between two conflicting emotions, relief and panic, and she was glad she was seated when she felt a terrifying weakness surging into her limbs.

'I don't know whether I ought to thank you or curse you,' she said through her clenched teeth, and Rafe's smile was no more than a cynical twist of the lips as he rose from his chair.

'Time will tell, Joceline.'

Jo was still sitting there in the hotel lounge long after Rafe had left, and she was aware only of the dull thudding of her heart at the bitter knowledge that she had sold herself for the sake of her family.

CHAPTER TWO

Jo WALKED across the carpeted floor on stockinged feet to stare disconsolately from her bedroom window at the grey morning light. A mantle of mist covered Table Mountain and it was raining. The rain had started the day before, and there was still no sign of the sky clearing.

A car passed in the street beyond the garden wall, its tyres on the wet tarmac churning up a spray of water, and Jo sighed unhappily as she leaned her hot forehead against the cool window-pane.

This was her wedding-day.

It had rained the first time she had married Rafe, but the sunshine of happiness had been in her heart. This time Jo felt as emotionally bleak as the weather, and when her breath misted the window-pane she turned back into the room to continue dressing.

The arrangements were that the marriage ceremony would take place in her home at ten o'clock that Saturday morning, and Jo was doing her best to remain calm, but with every passing second that well of anxiety inside her became more intense.

Dressed in her silky undergarments, she moved about the room with a natural, fluid grace. Her tall, slender figure was trapped every now and then in the full-length mirror against the wardrobe door, but Jo did not pause to admire her small-breasted, slim-waisted body with the nicely rounded bottom and long, shapely legs. Her hair, swept back into an attractive chignon, looked dark in the dreary light filtering in through the bedroom window, but on a clear day the sun could set fire to the rich auburn as easily as the carelessness of a junior nurse could set fire to her temper.

Jo slipped into the long-waisted, ivory-coloured dress with the puffy sleeves and scalloped neckline. Her hands went round to her back to pull up the zip, but just below her shoulder-blades it met with an obstruction.

'Damn!' she muttered irritably, her winged eyebrows almost meeting in a frown above slanted green eyes. She tugged at the zip, but it refused to budge in any direction, and she was becoming a little frantic when there was a knock on her bedroom door.

'Are you decent, Jo?' her brother demanded, opening the door slightly.

'I'm covered in all the right places, if that's what you mean,' she said, laughing mirthlessly. 'Please help me with this zip, Danny.' She turned her back on him the moment he entered the room and closed the door behind him. 'The metal catch will insist on hooking the material halfway up my back.'

It took no more than a few seconds for Danny to rectify the problem, and Jo barely had time to don a pleasant expression before he spun her round for his brotherly inspection.

'You look beautiful, Jo,' he said gravely, his hands resting on her shoulders. 'I think you're more beautiful now than the first time you married Rafe.'

'Thank you, Danny,' she murmured, her gaze lingering for a moment on the red carnation pinned to the lapel of his pale grey suit before she turned from him to seat herself in front of the dressing-table.

There was a stabbing pain in the region of her chest, but she dared not pause to analyse it. If she did she knew she would burst into tears, so she snapped on the light above the mirror and concentrated instead on applying the final touches to her make-up.

'Everything has worked out rather well, don't you think?' Danny took up a lounging position against the wardrobe from where he had an unobstructed view of his sister's attractive profile with the straight nose, generous mouth and firm chin. 'What I mean is,' he continued with a short laugh, 'who would have thought that the desperate circumstances that led to this meeting with Rafe would have made the two of you realise that you still love each other?' Danny was silent for a moment, then he asked unexpectedly, 'You do still love him, don't you, Jo?'

She picked up the single strand of pearls she had borrowed from her mother, and fastened it about her throat. It gave her time to think and to steady the anxious beat of her heart before she turned on the stool to face Danny with an outward calmness that hid the unhappy turmoil inside her.

'I never stopped loving Rafe,' she lied.

'Thank God for that!' Danny sighed audibly as he straightened himself from his lounging position against the wardrobe. 'I've had this horrible feeling all week that your decision to marry him again might have something to do with the loan. Ridiculous, isn't it?'

'Ridiculous,' she echoed, smiling, but Danny had hit on the truth with such an unexpected accuracy that her heart was beating nervously in her throat, and she quickly changed the subject. 'Where's Mum?'

'Downstairs with Rafe. And that reminds me,' he patted her shoulder in passing as he went to the door, 'the minister phoned to say he was on his way, so you'd better buck up.'

'I'm almost ready,' she said, her face a serene, smiling mask despite the fact that every nerve and muscle in her body had become painfully tense with growing anxiety. 'Just give me a few minutes to myself.'

Danny paused at the door to smile at her, then he raised his fingers to his forehead in a casual salute. 'I'll wait for you in the hall.'

Jo sagged physically and mentally the instant she was alone. If she had found the past few minutes of pretence exhausting, then how was she going to survive the next hour before she left with Rafe on that long car journey into the Karoo?

Her hand was shaking when she adjusted the light above the dressing-table mirror, but she had steadied herself when she picked up the sprig of imitation orange blossoms and pinned it to the side of the chignon at the back of her head.

I never stopped loving Rafe. Her reply to Danny's query drifted back into her mind. Why did she feel so uneasy about that lie? Was it because she was beginning to suspect she had spoken the truth?

Impossible! After their divorce Jo had forbidden the use of Rafe's name in her presence. She had picked up her nursing career where she had left off, and she had flung herself into her work with a vengeance. She had made every possible effort to put Rafe out of her mind and her heart, and she had succeeded. Hadn't she?

Jo couldn't be sure of this, but if her feelings for Rafe had remained unaltered, then this was the worst possible moment to make that discovery, because the Rafe Andersen she was marrying today was not the same man she had married almost four years ago. The man she was marrying today was a heartless replica, and he was demanding an equally heartless price for his generosity.

The past eight days had been a nightmare of working her notice at the hospital and feigning happiness to her family. Jo had to admit, though, that Rafe had made it easier for her by scheduling his visits to her home to coincide with the time when she would be away on duty at the hospital, and on the one occasion when they did meet it had been to select a wedding-ring and to confer with the officiating minister.

Jo stared long and hard at her image in the mirror. She had been adding an extra touch of blusher to her high cheekbones when she remembered how she had looked the first time she had married Rafe. Happiness had made her face glow and her eyes sparkle like jewels, but this time she had had to resort to the clever use of make-up to achieve a semblance of that happy look.

She had gone into marriage then with so many naïve, romantic notions, but this time there was only the harsh reality of what would be expected of her.

The sound of a car coming up the drive made her switch off the light above the dressing-table mirror. She sat there for a moment, listening to the rain dripping down the gutters, then she rose from the stool with a look of resignation on her face and slipped her stockinged feet into high-heeled shoes that matched the ivory colour of her dress.

'Ready or not, this is *it*, Jo,' she addressed herself through clenched teeth and, drawing a deep, steadying breath, she left her room and walked along the carpeted passage towards the stairs.

Danny was waiting down in the hall as he had promised, and he smiled up at her when she descended the last flight of stairs. Jo tried to smile back at him, but her facial muscles were too rigid with tension. He handed her a small bouquet of crimson carnations. Held against the pale ivory of her dress the flowers looked like splashes of freshly spilled blood.

How appropriate, she thought, swallowing convulsively to quell an unexpected wave of hysteria as Danny offered her his arm and opened the living-room door.

The murmur of conversation in the living-room ceased the moment Danny opened the door. There were no guests—Jo had insisted on this—and there was no wedding march, recorded or otherwise. She entered the room with Danny to a silence so intense that her nerves received a painful jar at the sound of a vehicle's safety siren going off in the street.

The Reverend Mr Stirk was a lean, balding man in his early fifties. He was standing beside the tall floral arrangement which had been delivered to the house shortly after breakfast that morning, and Lavinia Harris stood a little to his left, her pink corsage the only splash of colour on her pearl-grey outfit.

Jo was aware of their presence, but her glance was drawn irrevocably to the granite-hard features of the man in the dark, impeccably tailored suit who had turned to face the door when she had entered the room, and her knees threatened to buckle beneath her. The hand that Rafe held out to her was big, tanned, and callused with manual labour. Jo felt the roughness of his palm against hers and the crushing strength of his fingers. Suddenly she panicked.

Call it off! she wanted to shout. For pity's sake, let's call the whole thing off!

Her glance collided with Rafe's and she wondered what he was thinking, but his expression remained shuttered.

The marriage ceremony was brief, and their responses were prompted by the minister. 'With this ring I thee wed,' Rafe said when he slipped the wedding-band on to her finger, and Jo knew the claustrophobic sensation of a trapdoor being slammed shut, imprisoning her.

Mr Stirk concluded the ceremony with, 'Those whom God hath joined together let no man put asunder', then he cleared his throat and, looking embarrassed, added, 'I believe it's customary at a wedding of this private nature for the groom to kiss the bride.'

Jo shrank inwardly from this suggestion, and she was totally unresponsive when Rafe turned her towards him and tilted her face up for a kiss. His lips brushed against hers, their touch familiar, but cool and impersonal, and somewhere deep inside her a half-forgotten pulse was throbbing back to life.

No! Oh, please, God! No! she prayed silently and desperately while she responded like an automaton to her family's congratulations. Don't let me feel that way! Not after all these years!

It was some time later, when Lavinia and Danny were seeing Mr Stirk off the premises, that Rafe pinned Jo down with his dark gaze. He smiled twistedly as he came towards her, then he gestured with the glass of champagne in his hand. 'Shall we drink to a profitable union?'

'You mean a profitable *purchase*, don't you?' Her mask of serenity slipped momentarily to reveal her repugnance. 'You bought me, remember? The transaction has been signed and sealed. All that's left is for me to deliver. Not so, Rafe?'

His mouth thinned and a muscle twitched along the side of his square jaw. She had angered him—she recognised the signs—but his overall expression remained as inscrutable as before.

'I stand corrected.' His coldly dispassionate glance flicked over her. 'I shall drink instead to my latest and most profitable acquisition.'

Jo felt chilled and socially degraded as she watched him lift his glass to his lips and drain it in one gulp seconds before Lavinia and Danny returned to the living-room. Her palm had itched to strike Rafe, but her conscience had warned against it. She had provoked him deliberately, and that meant that she was partly to blame if he seemed bent on piling insult upon insult.

There was no time for Jo to change out of her dress into something more comfortable before they left. They had dallied too long over the champagne and the snacks, and she knew from experience that they would have to leave as soon as possible if they wanted to arrive at Satanslaagte before dark.

Jo was disengaging herself from her mother's tearful embrace when Rafe came in out of the rain after stowing the last of her belongings in the boot of his metallic green Mercedes. Raindrops glistened on his dark hair as he lowered his head to kiss Lavinia's proffered cheek, but when he shook hands with Danny there was something in the look that passed between them that puzzled Jo briefly.

Some moments later Jo was seated in the car beside Rafe and being driven down the circular driveway towards the gate. She glanced back at the house and wished herself back in the safety of her room above the portico where Lavinia and Danny stood waving. Jo waved back with a hollow feeling in her chest, then she settled back in her seat and stared straight ahead of her at the wipers swishing back and forth across the windscreen while they headed towards the dual carriageway which would link them up with the road to Beaufort West.

The rain eased down to a fine drizzle on the N1 once they were beyond the towering peaks of the Du Toits mountain range and had driven through the lush Hex River valley where the winter cold had stripped the vines bare in the vineyards. Rafe had maintained a brooding silence in the car since they had left Cape Town, but Jo welcomed it. She was in no mood for idle conversation, and it suited her that they spoke to each other only when it was absolutely necessary.

They stopped for a light lunch at a hotel in the small town of Touws River which had once been an important railway junction, and it was when they continued their journey an hour later that the sun finally began to emerge behind the clouds. The gleam of gold on Jo's finger captured her attention, and she found herself remembering a conversation she had had with her brother not more than a month ago.

'How would you feel if Rafe had to walk through that door unexpectedly?' Danny had asked one evening when she had arrived home late and was warming a glass of milk for herself in the kitchen.

'Scared,' she had answered him with an honesty born of surprise.

'Why would you be scared?'

'I loved him once, and I'd be scared that he might somehow stir up those old feelings only to throw them back in my face,' she had said.

'Would you marry him again if he should ask you?' Danny had persisted.

'Rafe would never ask me to marry him again, and I swear I shall never set foot on Andersen soil again even if Rafe should come to me on bended knees.'

Jo had been wrong on two counts. Rafe did ask her to marry him again, and he had not needed to go down on bended knees to get her to accept. Marriage to Rafe was the condition to the loan Danny needed, and before long she *would* set foot on Andersen soil again. Jo dreaded the thought, and she dreaded also the cold-blooded demands Rafe would be making on her.

'Are we going to drive all the way to the Satanslaagte without speaking to each other?' demanded Rafe as they entered Laingsburg's municipal boundary.

'What is there to say?' she demanded in response as she turned slightly towards him and eased her legs into a more comfortable position.

'I can think of quite a few things to say.'

'That's odd.'

That unaccustomed ring of sarcasm in her voice did not escape Rafe and he slanted a quick, frowning glance at her. 'What's odd about it?' he wanted to know.

'You never used to be talkative.'

'People change.' Rafe's hand brushed accidentally against her knee when he shifted down to a lower gear, and an electrified sensation shot up along Jo's thigh. 'I know *I* have changed.'

'You can say *that* again,' she responded bitingly, her body still tingling with the unnerving sensation his touch had aroused when they entered Laingsburg and drove slowly past the steepled church that dated back to 1883.

Jo laced her fingers together in her lap in an attempt to maintain her outwardly calm appearance, but the feel of that gold wedding-band on the finger of her left hand was making her heart take a frantic, suffocating leap into her throat as her mind unwillingly took stock of the situation.

She had been married to Rafe before, and she had given herself to him in love. This time the ring on her finger was Rafe's seal of purchase, and he would be taking possession of her body for the sole purpose of making sure that she would, in time, fulfil her part of the bargain by producing an heir for Satanslaagte.

Satanslaagte. Valley of the devil. It was there where she had been taught the meaning of defeat, and she had left hating it as passionately as Rafe loved it. If she had had a choice she would never have returned, but she supposed there was some consolation in the knowledge that Averil Andersen would not be in residence for the next two months.

They were crossing the bridge over the dry Buffels River and leaving the town of Laingsburg behind them when Rafe resumed their conversation. 'You've changed too, Joceline.'

'Oh, for goodness' sake, Rafe, will you stop calling me *Joceline*?' she exclaimed with an irritation that stemmed from the distasteful, slightly panic-stricken thoughts flitting through her mind.

'I think Joceline suits the assertive image you've acquired. You never used to be that way before.'

'More's the pity!' she muttered to herself, but Rafe's soft, throaty laughter made her realise that he had heard her.

'I couldn't agree more,' he mocked her. 'That flash of assertive anger in your eyes adds an exciting and alluring spark to your beauty. It also makes you much more desirable.'

Jo stiffened and slanted an angry glance at Rafe's stern, ruggedly handsome profile, but her acid response died a sudden death on her lips as his dark eyes met and held hers for a breathtaking instant.

'You always were desirable, Jo.' There was something in the deep timbre of his voice that sent a flurry of tremors along her nervous system. 'That's one thing that never changed when we were married before.'

Jo altered her position slightly and stared fixedly out of the window beside her. She wished she could refute his statement, but she couldn't. Rafe had not touched her during those final days after he had moved out of the room they had shared, but the desire had been there in his eyes whenever she had caught him staring at her.

She thrust aside these memories which persisted in crowding her mind and tried instead to focus her attention on the passing scenery as they travelled deeper into the heart of the Karoo.

The Karoo was a vast, scrub-covered land which was dotted sparsely with clusters of pepper and acacia trees, and there was nothing to break the monotony of the journey except the occasional appearance of the flat-topped hills in the far distance. It was on this semi-desert land that farmers like Rafe grazed their wool-producing sheep and continued to fight their relentless battles against the ever-present threat of drought.

'Does your mother know that you've married me again?' she questioned Rafe when the soft drone of the car's engine threatened to put her to sleep.

'I sent her a cable.'

Jo glanced at his tight-lipped profile. 'Did you explain what prompted you to marry me again?'

'Did you tell your family that marrying me and having my child was the condition I stipulated for the loan?' he parried her query sharply.

'No.' She lowered her gaze briefly to those powerful hands resting on the steering-wheel and swallowed at the lump that had risen unexpectedly into her throat. 'I didn't want to upset them.'

'Exactly.'

Jo sighed inwardly with an odd feeling of relief. 'I'm glad you haven't lost the ability to care.'

'I care about a lot of things which you wouldn't know about.'

'Because I'm a city girl with no knowledge of the land?' she countered mockingly, and his jaw hardened with anger.

'Where you were born and bred is of no consequence. Knowledge is something one can acquire only if the interest is there.'

'So we're back to that, are we?' she retorted coolly, keeping a tight rein on her anger.

'Back to what?' he demanded, casting a frowning glance in her direction.

'I could adapt to living on a farm if I chose to apply myself.'

His expression became shuttered and he dismissed the subject with a decisive wave of his hand. 'I have no desire to rake up old, worn-out arguments.'

'Neither have I,' she finally confessed into a stony silence.

It was late afternoon, and Beaufort West lay a few kilometres up ahead of them. It was the largest town in the central Karoo, and the inhabitants often called it the 'oasis town'. It couldn't have been named more aptly. After the long drive through the hot, arid Karoo the town was a veritable oasis with its streets lined with pear and jacaranda trees, its green playing-fields and pretty gardens.

Jo could see the rooftops of buildings jutting out above the trees as they approached the outskirts of the town, and anxiety clutched at her throat like a vice. This was the second time in eight days that she was entering this picturesque town, where the quaint old shops with their zinc awnings and fancy wrought-iron work blended comfortably with the modern buildings which had been erected in recent years.

Satanslaagte lay about thirty kilometres to the north of Beaufort West. It took a twenty-minute drive along a winding dirt road to reach the farm, and Jo sat rigidly still beside Rafe as they sped past remembered landmarks. The Mercedes held the road firmly, ploughing up a cloud of dust behind it, and all too soon Rafe was swinging the car off the road to bring it to a halt in front of that familiar pillared gateway on which the name

'Satanslaagte—R. Andersen' had been freshly painted.

Rafe got out to open the gate, the first of several along the track leading up to the homestead. He drove through it, then he got out again and closed the gate before driving off.

Never leave a gate open behind you. That was the cardinal rule on a Karoo farm. Jo had found it odd until she discovered that the breeding of sheep for their wool was an intricate business which could cause severe financial losses if animals were allowed to stray at will into neighbouring camps.

Their arrival at Satanslaagte did not go unnoticed. Two black children ran barefooted like hares across the scrub-covered veld to attend to the last few gates, and Rafe pressed a couple of silver coins into their hands before the two little boys sped away again.

The fiery sun was sinking swiftly towards the flat-topped hills in the distance when Rafe drove up to the sprawling homestead surrounded by neatly trimmed lawns and tall, shady trees. It seemed like yet another cool green oasis in the scorching semi-desert, and it was all still so familiar to Jo that the past and the present came together in an agonising rush that made her draw a painful, shuddering breath.

'We're home,' Rafe announced, getting out of the car and walking round the bonnet to open the door for her.

Home? Satanslaagte never was, and never would be *home* to her, she was thinking cynically when she stepped from the car.

Jo was easing the stiffness out of her body after the long ride when a fully grown Alsatian appeared around the corner of the house. It barked once, a yelping bark, then bore down on her at a speed that made her catch her breath. She backed away nervously and collided with Rafe's solid chest. At any other time she might have leapt away to avoid the contact, but at that moment there was a feeling of safety in the steadying touch of those strong hands gripping her shoulders.

'Fritz!' The dog halted in its tracks at the sound of that sharp, commanding voice, and Rafe released Jo with a faintly derisive smile. 'Don't tell me you're also afraid of dogs?'

'Only when they charge at me with what appears to be vicious intent,' she defended herself with a forced calmness when that cold surge of fear finally subsided to leave her with a peculiar lameness in her limbs.

'In this instance Fritz's exuberance may be interpreted as a welcome.' Rafe summoned the Alsatian with a wave of his hand. 'I suggest you get acquainted.'

Jo extended her hand towards the animal. 'Hello, Fritz.'

The Alsatian approached her cautiously. He sniffed at her fingers, then he nudged her palm with his cold, wet nose as an indication that he wanted his head stroked, and Jo obliged by running her hand over his smooth coat and scratching him gently behind the ears.

'He likes you,' Rafe informed her.

Jo smiled naturally for the first time that day as she stooped over the animal. 'How long have you had Fritz?'

'Two years,' came the answer. 'He was a surprise birthday gift from Lorin.'

Lorin. There was the bitter taste of gall in Jo's mouth, and her smile faded long before she straightened to see a black man in khaki shirt and trousers walking towards them.

Jo recognised Stan at once. He had grown up on the farm with Rafe, and there was no one Rafe trusted more than his childhood friend.

Stan smiled and lifted his old felt hat in greeting. 'Hello, madam.'

'Hello, Stan.' Jo returned his smile warmly. 'How is Klara?'

'She is well, madam,' Stan assured her, visibly pleased that Jo had remembered his wife's name. 'She's expecting our fourth child in two months' time.'

'You may bring the suitcases inside, Stan,' Rafe intervened abruptly, passing the Mercedes keys on to Stan.

'Yes, Master Rafe.'

Jo had a strange feeling that Rafe had wanted to end her conversation with Stan before something was said between them which was not intended for her ears.

Don't be silly! she reprimanded herself silently, shivering in the coolness of the late afternoon air as Rafe ushered her towards the trellised stoep that ran along two sides of the house. It was then that

Jo noticed the building operations which were in progress on the east-facing side of the homestead.

'Are you making alterations to the house?' she asked curiously.

'I'm adding on a few extra rooms.'

That was odd! The original homestead was big enough to house almost a dozen people comfortably. Why would Rafe need these additional rooms?

Jo slanted a glance up at him, but there was something so forbidding about his stern profile that she decided to shelve the questions spinning through her mind as they entered the silent house and walked across the hall with its gleaming yellowwood floor.

Nothing had changed, she was thinking as Rafe guided her down the long, L-shaped passage which led to the bedrooms on the west side of the house. The wine-red carpet on the floor was what Averil Andersen had selected in preference to the mottled beige which Jo had believed would brighten up a passage which could be dark and dismal during certain times of the day. None of Jo's suggestions had ever met with her mother-in-law's approval, and in the end Jo had simply been too despondent to care.

She was trying to banish these memories from her mind when Rafe opened the door to the master bedroom, and her heart was thudding painfully against her breastbone as he drew her inside.

This was the room she had shared with Rafe. It was in this room that she had known her happiest as well as her most heartbreaking moments.

Jo pulled herself together with an effort to cast a critical glance about the spacious room with its walk-through dressing-room and adjoining bathroom.

It was not quite as she had remembered. The solid oak furniture had not changed, but she was pleasantly surprised to discover that the unsightly floral curtains across the sash windows had been replaced with a pale blue chintz to match the drapes on the four-poster bed. The serviceable olive-green carpet had also been removed, and in its place was a plush creamy-coloured carpet which had been laid wall to wall.

Rafe was lounging against the wall beside the mirrored dressing-table. He was observing her closely as if he expected some sort of reaction, and Jo nervously stated the obvious. 'You've made a few changes.'

'Do you like it?'

'It's very nice,' she admitted, trying to quell the nervous flutters at the pit of her stomach as she forced herself to meet his penetrating gaze. 'Is this your room?'

'This is *our* room,' he stated clearly so that there would be no misunderstanding, and something in her expression made his heavy eyebrows lift in cynical amusement. 'How else are you to provide me with an heir if we don't share the same room and the same bed?'

A rush of angry, embarrassed heat surged into her cheeks, but her scathing response had to be suppressed at the sound of footsteps approaching the room.

Stan entered the bedroom seconds later with a large suitcase in each hand and a smaller suitcase tucked under each arm. He deposited them at the foot of the bed and glanced enquiringly at Jo when he straightened. 'Shall I leave the suitcases here, madam?'

She nodded and smiled stiffly. 'Thank you, Stan.'

Rafe straightened from his lounging position against the wall the moment Stan left the room. 'I have a few things to see to before it's dark, so I'll leave you to get yourself settled before dinner,' he said, exchanging his dark jacket and grey silk tie for a serviceable fleece-lined jacket.

Jo felt her rigid control slipping the moment the door closed behind Rafe, and she was suddenly shaking so much that she knew she had to sit down before she fell down.

This was going to be worse than she had imagined, Jo was thinking as she lowered herself on to the stool in front of the dressing-table. There were so many bitter memories lurking in this room she had once shared with Rafe, and she cringed inwardly at the thought of what was still to come.

Oh, God! What am I going to do? How am I going to live through this?

She stared almost blindly at the suitcases Stan had stashed so neatly at the foot of the bed, and then she leapt purposefully to her feet.

Unpack! That's what you're going to do! Unpack your suitcases and keep yourself busy!

CHAPTER THREE

IT WAS dark outside. The sun had set more than an hour ago and the stars sparkled like clusters of diamonds against the velvet of the night sky.

Jo had forgotten how bright the night stars could be in the Karoo. She had also forgotten that the temperature at night could drop to freezing in the winter, and she shivered as she let the curtain fall back into place. Her silk dress might have been warm enough for Cape Town's wet winter weather, but it was totally inadequate for the biting cold of the Karoo nights, and she slipped her hands round to her back to resume her battle with that stubborn zip.

She had unpacked her suitcases and had stashed them away on a high shelf in the dressing-room. What she wanted now was a hot bath and a change of clothing, but her patience had become frayed to the point where she seriously considered the possibility of tearing the dress off her body if the zip did not come unstuck soon.

Moments later Jo pulled open the dressing-table drawer, and she was actually reaching inside for the scissors when there was a light tap on the bedroom door.

'Come in!' she called, her voice sharp with irritation, and an elderly black woman in a pink overall entered the room.

Elsie was not a stranger to Jo. She had worked for Averil Andersen for many years, preparing the meals and supervising the rest of the household staff according to Averil's instructions. Circumstances had previously prevented Jo from getting close to this woman. Was she a friend? Or ought Jo to see her as an enemy?

'May I bring you something to drink before dinner, madam?' Elsie enquired, her round face revealing nothing except the polite concern which one would reserve for strangers.

'I won't have anything now, thank you, Elsie, but I would appreciate it if you could help me with this zip.'

It was desperation which had driven Jo to make that request. She could not tell whether Elsie would consider it beneath her station to deliver this small personal service, but Elsie stepped forward amiably, her white starched apron crackling as she moved.

'I'll do that, Elsie,' a deep male voice halted the woman, and she retreated hastily, leaving the room and closing the door behind her.

Jo had spun round at the sound of Rafe's voice, and her heart was beating out a nervous tattoo against her ribs as she met his dark gaze.

For a big man Rafe had a surprisingly light step. That was something else she had forgotten, Jo realised as she watched him take off his fleece-lined jacket and drape it across the back of the armchair which had been re-upholstered in a cream and blue striped material to match the rest of the décor in the room.

'Turn around,' he instructed, stepping towards her, and Jo turned her back on him in silence.

She thought she had prepared herself for the touch of his hands, but she tensed when his fingers brushed against her skin, and that knot of anxiety at the pit of her stomach received a painful wrench. If his light, impersonal touch still had the ability to send her pulse-rate into a frenzy, then how was she going to deal with the situation when Rafe actually made love to her?

'Thank you,' she muttered when she felt the zip give way beneath his fingers.

She started to move away, but Rafe caught her by the shoulders and held her in such a way that she could not fail to feel the disturbing warmth of his body against her back.

'Jo...' His voice was a low, throaty murmur just above her left ear that sent shivers of apprehension up and down her spine. She sensed that he was about to say something of importance, and she waited, hardly daring to breathe, but then she could almost feel him change his mind. His fingers tightened briefly on her shoulders, then he released her and gave her a gentle push in the direction of the bathroom. 'I need a shower before dinner, so don't be too long in the bath.'

Jo did not risk a glance in Rafe's direction as she fled through the dressing-room into the bathroom. She wished she could have known what he wanted to say, but later, when she thought about it, she was convinced that there was nothing he could have said to alter the distasteful circumstances of this unwanted second marriage.

Rafe was at least considerate enough not to invade her privacy while she was taking a bath. He remained in the bedroom until she emerged, fully clothed, from the dressing-room, and only then did he rise from his lounging position in the armchair to go into the bathroom. His expression had been dark and brooding, and she felt a stab of uneasiness as she seated herself at the dressing-table to tend to her hair and her make-up.

Jo had never been afraid of Rafe before, but she was afraid of him now. Perhaps it would be more to the point to say that she feared for herself. There was a hardness in him which had not been there before; a calculated savagery which she sensed rather than saw, and she wondered what could have happened in the three years since their divorce to bring about this change in him.

The deep amber of her long-sleeved woollen dress matched that hint of fire that flashed in her hair as she brushed it beneath the light hanging from the ceiling above the dressing-table. She coiled her hair into a fresh chignon, and she was about to fasten a tear-shaped pearl on a gold chain about her neck when Rafe emerged from the dressing-room with a brown suede jacket hooked on the finger of one hand.

He had changed into beige corded trousers, and a fresh white shirt which he had left unbuttoned at his strong, sun-browned throat so that she could not fail to catch a glimpse of the dark hair curling against his chest.

'Let me help you,' he offered, flinging his jacket across the foot of the bed and coming up behind her when the remembered texture of his hair-roughened skin made her fingers tingle and fumble with the catch on the chain.

'I can manage,' she protested, but Rafe took the chain from her, and once again the light touch of those strong fingers against her skin sent a little shiver racing through her that affected the normal rhythm of her pulse.

'Who gave you this pendant?' he asked when he had secured the latch.

'It was a gift from a friend on my last birthday.'

'This friend of yours—male or female?' His eyes held hers compellingly in the mirror while he thrust his hands into his trouser pockets and rocked slightly on his heels.

'Male,' she answered him.

Rafe's mouth tightened into a thin, ominous line. 'Was he your lover?'

'No, he was not my lover.' She sounded cool, but Rafe's nearness and the familiar smell of his after-shave was beginning to have a disturbing and heated effect on her senses. 'My friend was a paraplegic and we used to enjoy each other's company.'

Rafe's eyes narrowed reflectively. 'Why do you speak of him in the past tense?'

'He committed suicide three months ago.'

'I'm sorry,' he said, turning away from her to shrug himself into his suede jacket, but Jo had glimpsed a flicker of compassion in his eyes, and her heart lifted a fraction at the thought that he might not have become quite as hard as she had imagined.

'I was sorry too,' she admitted quietly, the pain of that loss still very real to her as she slipped her feet into soft brown pumps and rose from the stool. 'I'm ready for dinner, if you are.'

Jo preceded Rafe from the bedroom and they walked down the dimly lit passage without speaking. In the spacious entrance hall they turned right into the dining-room where the long oval table had been set for two.

Against the snow-white tablecloth the polished silverware sparkled beneath the lights hanging low over the table, and against the inner wall stood the mirrored mahogany dresser which had been in the Andersen family for generations. It was a beautiful piece of furniture, and Jo refreshed her memory by allowing her glance to travel briefly over the intricately carved panels.

Rafe opened the bottle of champagne which had been waiting on ice for their arrival, and shortly afterwards Elsie brought in the soup tureen. Elsie had always served at the table—she had not trusted anyone else with this task—and Jo had to admit that she did it well.

The meal Elsie had prepared for them that evening was not elaborate, but it was wholesome. The creamy tomato soup was followed by tender lamb, fresh vegetables and a crispy salad. After the sponge-cake dessert they retired to the lounge across the hall, and Elsie served them their coffee in front of the stone fireplace where a log fire was crackling in the grate.

Everything in the lounge was still the same, but the position of the padded floral armchairs, the long sofa and the occasional tables had been altered in such a way that one could enjoy the warmth of the fire no matter where one happened to be sitting in the room.

Jo wondered how Averil had managed to overcome her aversion to altering anything in the house. Or was Rafe also responsible for these changes?

'Tell me about your paraplegic friend,' Rafe prompted long after they had had their coffee, and Jo was glad of this opportunity to drag her thoughts away for a moment from the painful and humiliating memories evoked by her surroundings.

'Tony Ribeiro.' The handsome features of a dark-haired, dark-eyed young man flashed before her mind's eye as she said his name, but she was unaware of the sad, slightly reminiscent smile curving her wide, generous mouth. 'It was a motorcycle accident in his teens that put Tony in a wheelchair.'

'How old was he when he died?'

'Twenty-seven.' Jo stared into the flames dancing in the grate, but she was remembering that morning three months ago when she had come off night duty at the hospital and some sixth sense had made her call in at Tony's flat to find him slumped in his chair with a bullet wound in his temple. 'He was a talented young man,' she explained, trying to shut out the horror of that memory. 'At twenty-two he had started a small business of his own, making guitars for collectors and artists who wanted something special, and Tony not only made guitars, he also played them . . . beautifully.'

'Why did he commit suicide?'

She looked at Rafe for the first time since he had started to question her about Tony. She looked at that long, healthy, muscular body lounging in the armchair facing hers, and she wondered if anyone who was not physically disabled would ever know what really went on in the mind of someone who had lost the use of two or more limbs.

'I don't know why he committed suicide. I don't think anyone will ever really know what had prompted him to take his own life,' she answered Rafe quietly. 'Tony had his moments of deep depression, but he was basically a well-adjusted young man. That's what I always believed, but there must have been something I missed, something I must have overlooked, and I still have nightmares about the fact that I might have been too stupidly blind to see when he was reaching out to me for help.'

'You can't go through life blaming yourself for his death,' Rafe expounded harshly. 'You weren't this fellow's keeper.'

'No, I wasn't his keeper,' she agreed readily, 'but I was his friend, and the person he confided in the most.'

Rafe's dark, narrowed gaze held hers for interminable seconds before he got up to select one of the straight-stemmed pipes on the stand that stood on the mantelshelf.

'Would you mind if I smoked?' he asked unexpectedly, gesturing with the pipe in his hand.

'I don't mind, but smoking is bad for your health.'

He unzipped the tobacco pouch which had lain on the mantelshelf beside the pipe stand, and dipped the bowl of his pipe into it. 'You told me that once before.'

'I'm surprised you remembered,' she countered stiffly, her glance drawn to those big, long-fingered hands with the neatly clipped nails.

Rafe had strong hands, hands which she knew could bend a piece of metal into whatever shape he required, but Jo could recall only their gentleness whenever he had touched her. The memory of shared intimacies skipped unbidden through her mind, quickening her pulses, and her nerves flared uncomfortably when Rafe struck a match and held the flame over the bowl of his pipe.

'There are many things I remember about you,' he said, his dark, brooding gaze shifting over her while he lit his pipe.

Jo had an unnerving feeling that his thoughts had wandered along the same path as her own when their glances met and held, but he did not elaborate on his statement, and neither did she want him to. She could feel her cheeks stinging when she finally wrenched her gaze from his, and she prayed that he would blame her heightened colour on the warmth of the fire. He flicked the match into the grate and returned to his chair.

The pleasant aroma of Rafe's particular brand of pipe tobacco drifted towards her, and she realised suddenly that she had never been alone with him like this before. His mother had always been there, but Jo had had no argument with that. She could accept Averil Andersen's disapproving presence in the evenings, but not when Averil had openly joined forces with Lorin Scheepers to make Jo's life a misery, and Lorin had stayed to dinner on so many occasions that Jo had begun to think she might as well move in permanently.

Their bedroom had eventually been the only place where Jo could be truly alone with her husband, but it was during those infrequent moments of togetherness that the visible strain of her existence had finally led to Rafe accusing her of not making an effort to adapt. That had hurt, and it had hurt even more when her silence had been taken as a sign of guilt.

It had been wrong of her to remain silent. She should have voiced her grievances instead of bottling them up inside for fear of causing friction in the home, but wisdom had come too late, and there was nothing she could do now to alter the course of past events.

'More champagne?' Rafe got up to pour the remaining contents of the bottle into their glasses. 'I believe we have cause for a celebration, don't you?'

Jo sat rigidly on the edge of her chair, staring down at the glass he placed in her hand, and she realised that her mental stamina had waned along with the fizz in the champagne. 'I don't feel very much like celebrating.'

Rafe's eyebrows lifted in sardonic amusement above mocking eyes as he lowered his tall, muscular frame into his chair. 'Don't you think that the assured future of Harris Construction is something worth drinking a toast to?'

'At this very moment I wish Harris Construction never existed!' The words came out in a hiss through her teeth, and she was suddenly so cold that she put down her glass and rose from her chair to stand in front of the fire.

The long hand of the wall-clock above the mantelshelf was moving towards the half-hour. It was almost nine-thirty, and the tensions of the day were beginning to take their toll on Jo. Her control was slipping, and her calmness was deserting her to leave her panic-stricken at the knowledge that she had tied herself to Rafe to give him the child he had demanded in exchange for the financial security of her family. This was going to be such a heartless union that it terrified her just to think of it.

'I can't go through with this, Rafe.' Her hands gripped the mantelshelf, her knuckles whitening as she spoke. 'I know what I agreed to, but I—I can't.'

He could not have missed that pleading note in her voice, but he chose to ignore it. 'You *can* and you *will*!'

'It's all very well for you to insist, but you didn't have to——' The angry words jelled on her lips when she turned and saw the relentless hardening of his square jaw.

'I didn't have to...*what*?' Rafe demanded softly, dangerously.

'You didn't have to—to sell your body to save your family from the financial gallows,' she managed to complete her sentence in a choked voice.

'It was your choice,' he reminded her with a bluntness that made her wince inwardly.

'But I didn't have much of a choice, *did* I?'

'No, admittedly you didn't,' he agreed, sucking on his pipe with an enviable calmness and puffing out a cloud of aromatic smoke while his narrowed gaze lingered for a moment on the agitated rise and fall of her breasts. 'We were married before, Joceline. We're not total strangers to each other, so why should the thought of sharing my bed and having my child repel you?'

Jo shuddered inwardly and turned once again to face the warmth of the crackling fire in the grate. 'It's all so cold-blooded and calculated.'

'There's nothing cold-blooded and calculated about making love, Joceline.'

The desire to laugh was propelled by a rising wave of hysteria, and she clenched her hands at her sides until her nails bit painfully into her palms with the effort to control herself. 'We will be having sex for the sake of reproduction,' she corrected him coldly. 'If that isn't cold-blooded and calculated, then I'd like to know what is.'

Rafe did not contradict her.

Later, when Jo was preparing for bed, she wondered if a denial, however false, would not have been preferable to that frightening silence which had followed her statement.

She fastened the belt of her white towelling robe about her waist and seated herself on the padded stool in front of the dressing-table. Her insides were knotted with anxiety as she removed the pins from her hair and shook it free to fall in lustrous waves to her shoulders. She was reaching for her brush when the sound of approaching footsteps halted the action, and her heart took a frightened, agonising leap into her throat.

The nightmare was about to begin. It was a nightmare of her own choice, and there was no way that she could escape it.

She picked up her brush with a hand that shook visibly and she was brushing her hair with a vigour born of desperation when Rafe finally entered the bedroom and closed the door firmly behind him.

Jo did not look at him. She did not have to. She was aware of him with every quivering nerve in her body when he took off his jacket and came up behind her. His masculine image joined hers in the mirror and, without speaking, he took the brush from her seemingly nerveless fingers and pulled it through her hair.

He had performed this task for her many times during those six months they had been married, but in this instance the familiarity of his actions did not ease that terrible tension inside her. He eventually discarded the brush and combed his fingers through her hair as if he loved the feel of its silky texture. That, too, was a familiar experience, and so was that pleasant tingling sensation against her scalp.

'Your hair is shorter than it used to be, but it's still just as beautiful.'

Jo did not say anything. She merely sat there staring at him with her hands lying limply in her lap. She was praying silently for a reprieve, but she knew she would simply have to resign herself to the inevitable when those dark, smouldering eyes met hers in the mirror.

An odd sensation spiralled through her when he drew her to her feet, and it left her with a feeling of deadly calm. Was she calm? Or had she somehow lost the ability to feel anything?

Rafe's arm was about her waist, his hand settling in the hollow of her back to draw her up against his hard body, while his free hand cupped her chin and tilted her face up to his. His dark, searching gaze held hers for a moment, then he lowered his head and set his mouth on hers.

Jo held herself perfectly still. She was neither accepting nor rejecting the passionate demand his mouth was making on hers, and she was beginning to congratulate herself on her control when Rafe's head jerked up.

'What is this, Jo?' he demanded harshly, his expression dark and dangerous. 'Passive acceptance?'

Her features remained composed, but there was a flash of defiance in her green eyes. 'I'll give you the child you want, Rafe, but don't expect more from me than that.'

'If you think I'm going to have you lying supine in my arms when I know that you're capable of a passionate response, then you can think again, Joceline.'

'Whatever I might have felt for you four years ago is no longer there.'

'I wouldn't bet on that if I were you,' he snarled, his arm tightening about her waist like a vice.

The look on his face frightened Jo. She turned her head away to avoid his descending mouth, but his hand bunched into a fist in the hair at the nape of her neck, and her head was jerked back with a savage tug.

A cry of pain escaped her, and his mouth descended at that moment, stifling her cry to capture her parted lips. He thrust his tongue into her mouth in an erotic exploration of its tender moistness, and the world suddenly seemed to start spinning on its axis.

Jo could not remember exactly what happened after that, but Rafe's hands seemed to be everywhere, disrobing her and ripping off her flimsy nightdress. Somehow he also managed to discard his own clothes, and the shock of his naked flesh against hers sent a terrible weakness surging into her limbs. She had never known him to behave like this—his aggression was frightening—and Jo heard her own scream of terror as if it had come from someone else's throat as he flung her on to the fourposter bed and imprisoned her there with the weight of his heated, aroused body.

There was nothing gentle about the way Rafe was making love to her. There was a barely controlled savagery in the touch of his mouth and his hands on her body, but deep down inside her a pulse was beginning to throb in response, and she despised herself for not being able to control it.

Oh, God ... help me!

Jo tried to convince herself that she hated what he was doing to her, but she couldn't. He was igniting fires inside her which had lain dormant for far too long, and she was aching for him to fill that void inside her when he finally parted her thighs and thrust himself into her.

She could not believe that she was actually enjoying this physical union. Rafe wasn't making love to her, he was assaulting her, and yet her body was moving with his in that passionate, primitive rhythm of love. Her senses were filled with the exciting taste and smell of him, and she was no longer pushing at his hard, hair-roughened chest, but clinging to his wide shoulders in mindless surrender to the pleasure he aroused.

'No! Oh, *no!*' she groaned when she felt that sweet, aching tension inside her rising to a near-intolerable dimension in its search for fulfilment.

Rafe paused for a moment, his breathing ragged and the muscles in his powerful body quiveringly taut. His eyes looked glazed with desire, and they were so dark that they were almost black when he slid his hands beneath her bottom for a deeper penetration, then he delivered them both with a few quick, savage thrusts.

Jo lay limp and gasping for breath beneath the sagging, shuddering weight of Rafe's body while those waves of exquisite sensations subsided inside her. Rafe's laboured breath fanned her throat as he nuzzled her hair, and it was a long time before the wild hammering of their hearts slowed down to a more comfortable pace.

Sanity returned slowly and painfully, bringing with it a sweeping surge of burning shame. Her body, so long denied, had betrayed her, and she despised herself for allowing herself to succumb to that driving, physical need that Rafe had aroused in her. It had left her body sated, but mentally she felt used and so terribly empty.

Rafe eased himself away from her, and reached down to draw the duvet over them. They lay side by side for a long time, neither speaking nor touching, then he lifted himself up on to one elbow and leaned over her.

'Do you still say that what you felt for me before is no longer there?' he demanded, his smile mocking and openly triumphant.

'*Damn* you, Rafe!' Jo felt like striking him. She could take almost anything, but not his gloating manner in the face of her most humiliating defeat. '*Damn* you to *hell*, Rafe Andersen!'

'For what?' His eyebrows rose quizzically while he brushed a heavy strand of hair away from her flushed cheek and lightly trailed the back of his fingers along her throat to her shoulder. 'Are you damning me for proving that I can still make you want me?'

'Leave me alone!' she said fiercely, brushing off his hand and turning away from him to lie on the edge of the bed, facing the window.

'I'll leave you alone.' He laughed softly as he moved away from her to switch off his bedside light. For now.'

Jo switched off her own light. She welcomed the darkness, and tried desperately to find forget-fulness in sleep, but she was still awake an hour later, listening to Rafe's deep, even breathing.

For now! The words echoed repeatedly through her mind. Rafe had said that he would leave her alone...for now! This was just the beginning. That was what he had meant, and Jo wondered how she was going to survive all those days and nights ahead of her without losing what little self-respect and pride she still had left.

CHAPTER FOUR

AFTER lying awake for most of the night it was not
surprising that Jo slept late the Sunday morning,
but that was something she rarely did, and she felt
guilty that something like that could have happened to her on her first morning at Satanslaagte.

No one slept late on the farm—everyone was
always up at the crack of dawn—and Jo could well
imagine the scathing remark Averil Andersen would
have passed if she had been there.

Elsie was straightening from sliding a baking
sheet into the oven when Jo entered the kitchen,
and the woman's face was a polite mask as she took
off her oven mitts and smoothed the white apron
she wore over her pink overall.

'Good morning, Elsie.' Jo smiled, but she felt
wary and faintly embarrassed. 'I'm afraid I
overslept.'

'Master Rafe said not to wake you.'

How thoughtful of him! Jo was smiling cynically
when she encountered Elsie's questioning glance.

'Shall I make you something to eat for breakfast,
madam?'

Breakfast? Jo's stomach rejected the thought of
food, and she shook her head. 'A cup of tea would
do fine, thank you, and I'll have it out on the stoep.'

Elsie's dark gaze skimmed briefly over Jo's
slender frame in beige trousers, blue knitted sweater

and comfortable shoes with low, sturdy heels. She looked absolutely outraged at the thought that Jo could start the day without a decent breakfast, and Jo could not help smiling when she saw Elsie shaking her head disapprovingly as she turned away to switch on the electric kettle.

Jo wandered out on to the stoep and stood with her hands resting lightly on the trellised railings while she breathed in the clean, fresh Karoo air. Fritz, the Alsatian, lay stretched out in the sun below the steps leading down into the garden. He lifted his head and yawned as he made eye contact with Jo, then his head flopped down again between his paws and he promptly went to sleep. Fritz didn't have a care in the world, and Jo wished she could have changed places with him at that moment.

Beyond the garden with its sloping lawns, shady trees and neatly trimmed privet hedges lay the open veld where Rafe grazed his merino sheep.

Rafe! Jo's gaze settled disconsolately on the distant hills. She had lain awake for so many hours, trying to come to terms with the humiliating defeat she had suffered at his hands and wondering about the change in him. He had been brutal with her, as if he had been driven by a deep-seated anger, and Jo could not decide whether that anger had been directed at her personally, or if he had merely used her as an instrument on which he could vent his explosive feelings.

The sound of a step behind her scattered the troubled thoughts milling through her mind and she turned sharply to see Elsie placing a tray of tea on the glass-topped cane table.

'Is there anything else I can get you, madam?'

'No, thank you, Elsie.' Jo's smile was reassuring when she glimpsed a flash of concern in the dark eyes observing her so intently. 'When I've had my tea I might take a walk up on to that koppie behind the house to stretch my legs, and if Master Rafe should return before I do, then you may tell him where I am.'

Elsie nodded and left, and Jo helped herself to a cup of strong tea before she settled herself comfortably in one of the cane chairs.

She drank her tea and stared out across the well-kept garden. Her eyes were on the border of yellow shamrocks, but her mind was elsewhere. Is this how I'm going to spend my days? she asked herself. Am I going to have nothing to do in between meals other than to sit on the stoep and sip tea? No! Not again!

Jo finished her tea quickly and took the tray through to the kitchen. The screen door slammed shut behind her when she stepped outside, and she could feel Elsie's curious glance following her as she was striding out across the yard. Her pace was brisk, and she was approaching the shearing shed before she realised that Fritz had followed her silently and was padding along beside her.

'Thanks, Fritz.' She smiled wanly at the Alsatian as they passed the shearing shed. 'I could do with a friend right now!'

The koppie rose out behind the stables, and it was a steep climb up on to the crest of the small hill, but Jo had always enjoyed the view from there. Her heart was pounding in her chest, and the blood was singing in her veins when she finally lowered herself on to a flat boulder to catch her breath. She had always felt purged and ready to battle with her problems after the stiff climb to the top of the koppie. She felt that way again now as she sat there scanning the distant horizon.

Rafe's land stretched almost as far as the eye could see. Sheep were grazing in the camps, or gathering around drinking troughs, but as the middle of the day approached they would seek shade beneath the acacia trees that dotted the sparse vegetation of the Karoo.

There were two men on horseback in one of the camps to the far north. They were two unidentifiable black spots moving slowly across the shimmering, scrub-covered earth, but Jo knew it would be Rafe and Stan.

What did they do when they rode out like that? Count the sheep? Check the fences? The questions racing through her mind made her realise how unenlightened she was about the activities on a sheep farm. It also made her pause to review her own situation. Could she spend the rest of her life with a man who didn't love her? Could she bear him a child to fulfil her part of the agreement, and then renounce her flesh and blood in order to gain her freedom? A blade of dry grass snapped between her agitated fingers.

'Whether you like it, or not, Rafe Andersen, you're going to be stuck with me for life.' Jo spoke her thoughts out aloud to the semi-desert landscape spread out before her. 'If I'm to have your child, then I'm staying on at Satanslaagte to nurse it into adulthood.'

But where would she stand? What would her position be in this household? What, exactly, did Rafe expect of her? She hadn't asked, and he hadn't said, but it was something she had to know!

'Come on, Fritz, it's time to go.'

The dog responded to her call and halted his mad chase after a grasshopper to bound down the hill ahead of her.

Despite Jo's misgivings, Rafe did come home for lunch. She heard Fritz bark a greeting, and her heart seemed to turn over in her breast when Rafe finally walked into the dining-room.

It was a painfully familiar sight to see this big, ruggedly handsome man dressed in khaki and dusty suede boots. The smell of the sun and the veld clung to him, it quivered in her sensitive nostrils to awaken unbidden memories, and she had difficulty ridding herself of that aching tightness in her throat.

Rafe joined her at the table and helped himself to cold ham and salads. 'I trust you slept well?' he asked with that hateful hint of mockery in his dark eyes.

'I did, thank you,' she answered him stiffly, averting her gaze and attacking the food on her plate with an enthusiasm that stemmed from embarrassment rather than hunger.

'Your face looks sunburnt,' he observed while they ate their meal. 'Did you spend some time out in the sun this morning?'

'I went for a walk up on to the koppie.'

'That's rather a steep climb.'

'I know, but I enjoyed the exercise and I always did like the view from up there.'

Rafe looked up from his plate, his eyebrows raised in a questioning arc above his eyes. 'You've been up there before?'

'Many times.' She put down her knife and fork and dabbed at her mouth with her table napkin. 'Why should that surprise you?'

'You dislike the Karoo, and yet you tell me you climbed the koppie this morning because you've always liked the view from up there.'

'I don't dislike the Karoo. What did I say or do to give you that impression?'

Rafe didn't answer her. He was staring at a point somewhere beyond her left shoulder, and the look of fury that distorted his features made her shrink from him inwardly if not physically.

What had she said to make him so angry?

The visible signs of anger faded, but the tension remained until Elsie brought in their tea and cleared the table.

'We must talk, Rafe,' Jo said quietly when they were alone. 'I need to know what you expect of me.'

'I expect to have you in my bed at night.'

She forced herself to remain calm while she fought down a wave of resentment and anger. 'You've already made that perfectly clear, but it still leaves me with a tremendous amount of time on my hands.'

'Ours is not a conventional marriage, so that leaves us both free to live our lives as we choose and separate from one another.'

'Damn it, Rafe, stop pretending you don't know what I'm talking about!' she rebuked him sharply. 'I want to know where I stand in this house!'

Rafe's eyes held hers as he swallowed down a mouthful of tea, then he smiled twistedly. 'You may consider yourself mistress of this house for as long as you choose to stay, and whether you make it your home or your prison will be entirely up to you.'

Jo was beginning to see a glimmer of light at the end of this particular tunnel, but she had to be sure. 'In other words,' she began warily, 'I may do whatever I please, and I may make whatever changes I wish in the house as long as it doesn't interfere with the way you choose to live your life?'

'Exactly!' The word seemed to come out on a bark before he drained his cup and pushed back his chair to rise from the table. 'Excuse me, I have work to do.'

Jo scarcely dared to breathe as she watched him stride out of the dining-room. She heard him crossing the hall and moments later a door slammed in the house.

Rafe had gone into his study. This was his private sanctum, and no one, not even Jo, had been allowed to go in there without being invited. That was what Averil Andersen had said, and Jo had taken it for granted that the instruction had come direct from Rafe, but, in retrospect, she doubted it. Averil had done everything within her power to limit the time Jo could have had alone with Rafe, and barring her from entering Rafe's study had been no more than a ruse.

Jo finished her tea and took the tray through to the kitchen before she went to her room. Her mind was wide awake, but she felt extraordinarily tired as she closed the bedroom door behind her and kicked off her shoes. She exchanged her trousers and knitted sweater for a towelling robe, and stretched herself out on the bed in an attempt to relax. The past ten days had been physically and mentally taxing, and all she needed was to get some rest.

The Sunday afternoon silence in and around the farm house was druggingly intense and she actually dozed off, but she surfaced half an hour later to hear water running in the bathroom. She realised that it had to be Rafe taking a shower, but the thought did not alarm her.

She somehow went to sleep again, and the next time she awoke she found Rafe standing beside the bed, the whiteness of the towel draped about his lean hips contrasting heavily with the tanned, muscular fitness of his otherwise naked body. His hair was damp and combed back severely from his broad forehead, and there was something in the way he looked at her that stirred a half-forgotten memory, but that look was gone before Jo could analyse it.

He lifted a knee on to the bed and then he was leaning over her, imprisoning her with a hand on either side of her body. Her pulses fluttered a little wildly, and her gaze left his only to travel across his wide shoulders and down along his hair-roughened chest to his taut, flat stomach.

'Leave me alone, Rafe,' she pleaded huskily, the clean male smell of him stirring her senses while that aura of raw masculinity aroused a primitive and deeply feminine desire to submit to his male dominance.

'I wish I could leave you alone,' he growled, 'but I've been thinking about you all morning, and I can't shake the memory of how good you felt in my arms last night.'

'Oh, *please*!' Her cheeks flamed with embarrassment and she pushed at his arms in an attempt to get away, but he straddled her body and undid the belt of her robe before she could stop him. 'Don't, Rafe! Please *don't*!'

Her plea went unnoticed, and a wave of helplessness surged through her. To resist would result in an undignified brawl from which she knew she would emerge the loser, and she stilled unwillingly beneath him while he took off her robe and slid it out beneath her. Rafe's fingers were deft as he undid the front catch of her bra, and the flimsy garment followed the same path as her robe. The only thing left was the triangle of lace covering the most intimate part of her body, but she was soon stripped of that too.

'It's been a long time.' His eyes devoured her while he drew the pins from her hair, and he combed his fingers gently through it before his hands acquainted themselves once again with the womanly contours of her body. 'I've been starved too long, and I'm hungry for you, Jo.'

'Oh, God!' His touch was sending little shafts of unwanted pleasure cascading through her, and the words left her lips on a groan. 'I hate you for doing this to me, Rafe!'

'I know you hate me, but I also know I can still make you want me, so...' His smouldering glance held hers while he whipped off his towel and lowered himself on to her. 'Don't fight it this time, Jo,' he murmured, taking her mouth in a drugging kiss.

She didn't fight it. She couldn't. Not when he was arousing those delicious fires which only he could assuage completely. There was no point in pretending that she did not want him. Her mind might continue to deny it, but her body would betray her every time, and she knew she would simply have to learn to live with that humiliating fact. He could know that she wanted him, but he must never know that she still loved him. Never! She would rather die than let him see into her heart again.

Jo worked out a comfortable routine for herself during the next three weeks to keep herself occupied, while also giving herself time to pursue her own interests. Initially she encountered a certain amount of opposition from the staff when she stepped in and took charge of the house and the garden, but she soon won them over with her patience and understanding.

Her Volkswagen Jetta had arrived by rail during her first week at Satanslaagte, and it had felt good to be mobile again. Rafe had transferred the first instalment of a monthly allowance into her bank account. Jo had discovered this on her first trip to town, but money was still a touchy subject with her, and she had delved into her own savings to purchase a few items she had required.

She had also bought a few crochet needles and cotton. Crocheting was an enjoyable pastime, and it was something she could pick up and put down without losing the basic thread of what she was doing. What she had not expected was that the staff's interest in her crocheting would result in a twice-weekly homecraft class for the wives of the farm labourers.

Elsie had been the first to ask Jo if she would teach her to crochet, and then—one by one—the others had come. By the end of Jo's third week at Satanslaagte she was teaching six women to crochet, as well as knit, and they had arranged to get together twice a week, in the afternoon, under the shady oak behind the house.

It was during Jo's fourth week on the farm that Lorin Scheepers put in her first appearance. Jo was having tea out on the front stoep on the Wednesday afternoon when a dusty BMW sped up to the house and stopped close to the steps with an abruptness that made the tyres skid on the gravel.

Jo rose to her feet, recognising the driver as Lorin before she got out of the car. Fritz recognised her as well. The Alsatian ran forward, eager for a pat, but Lorin leapt past him on to the shady stoep as if he did not exist, and Fritz padded back to Jo's side with a soft whine of disappointment in his throat.

Lorin hadn't changed. The dark hair was still tied back into that casual pony-tail, and there was still that enviable buoyancy in her step when she walked.

Long dark lashes framed crystal-clear blue eyes, and they flashed at Jo with that well-remembered look of disdain in their depths.

Jo stood silent and erect while Lorin dug her fingers into the pockets of her tight-fitting khaki trousers and leaned back against the trellised railing to cross one dusty riding boot over the other.

'I honestly didn't think Rafe would be crazy enough to want to marry you again, but...' beneath the brown shirt Lorin's slim shoulders lifted in a shrug '...I guess that's his business.'

That was typical of Lorin. She did not waste time on polite preliminaries and went straight in to the attack. Someone really ought to teach her manners, Jo was thinking as she gestured calmly towards the tray. 'May I offer you a cup of tea?'

Lorin waved aside Jo's invitation. 'This isn't a social visit. My parents sent me to ask if you and Rafe would join us for dinner this coming Friday evening. It's my father's sixtieth birthday and they're having a couple of friends over.'

'I'll mention it to Rafe.'

Lorin turned to leave, but she paused at the top of the steps to subject Jo to another contemptuous stare. 'You didn't fit in before, so what makes you think that you'll fit in now?'

It was at this point that Fritz seemed to sense the animosity between the two women and, shifting closer to Jo's side, he let out a low, throaty growl. Jo placed a silencing hand on the Alsatian's ruff and forced a smile to her lips. 'I'll let you know as soon as I've discovered the answer for myself.'

Lorin's gaze dropped briefly to the animal at Jo's side, and a faintly malevolent smile lifted the corners of her beautiful mouth. 'I'd appreciate it if you'd tell Rafe that I'll meet him at the usual place tomorrow,' she said.

Jo's breathing felt restricted, as if her lungs had suddenly been clamped in a vice, but outwardly she remained calm and composed. 'I'll tell him,' she promised, her glance steady.

Fritz relaxed his guard and lay down again beside Jo's chair as Lorin sped away from the house, but for Jo it took a little longer to rid herself of the tension gripping her insides.

She sat down heavily, her hands clenching the arms of the cane chair. The usual place? Where was the usual place? And why did Rafe and Lorin meet each other there?

Fritz stirred beside her and sat up with a little whine of excitement in his throat as Rafe approached them from the east side of the house.

'Traitor,' Rafe muttered accusingly, leaning down to give Fritz an affectionate pat before he took off his wide-brimmed safari hat and helped himself to a cup of tea. 'Was that Lorin I saw leaving?' he asked over his shoulder.

'Yes.' The word came out in an angry hiss, but Jo controlled herself instantly. 'Her parents sent her over to invite us to dinner this coming Friday evening. I believe it's her father's sixtieth birthday.'

'Did you accept?'

'I said I'd speak to you first.' She wished he would sit down while he drank his tea instead of towering over her and giving her a crick in the neck.

'I imagine it's time we started accepting invitations as well as issuing a few of our own to the neighbours.'

It was all a terrible farce. After nearly four weeks of marriage Rafe considered it was time they went on display to the public as a happily married couple. But it was all a *lie*! Jo wanted to laugh, but she hastily curbed the feeling for fear she might end up crying.

She got up slowly and walked a few paces away from Rafe towards the variegated ivy ranking along one end of the trellised stoep. It helped to quell that feeling of hysteria inside her.

'Lorin asked me to give you a message.' She welcomed the warmth of the afternoon sun against her back when she turned to face Rafe. 'She said she would meet you tomorrow at the usual place.'

Rafe inclined his head briefly to acknowledge the message, but his expression did not alter while he finished his tea and placed his empty cup on the tray.

'I'll be a little late for dinner this evening,' was all he said as he picked up his hat and walked off in the same direction he had come earlier.

Jo watched with mixed feelings as he disappeared around the corner of the house. She was disappointed, angry, hurt and—she might as well admit it—*jealous*! She had no right to expect an explanation, but she had hoped he would give her one out of courtesy, if nothing else.

'Is Miss Lorin having dinner here this evening?' Elsie wanted to know when Jo carried the tea tray into the kitchen.

'I didn't invite her.' There was a hint of defiance in Jo's manner as she placed the tray on the well-scrubbed table where Elsie sat peeling potatoes.

'It's time Miss Lorin found herself a husband of her own instead of running after——'

'Instead of running after Master Rafe?' Jo filled in for her when she broke off abruptly with an embarrassed look on her face. 'Is that what you were going to say, Elsie?'

'I'm sorry, madam.'

'You don't have to apologise.' Jo's thoughtful gaze followed the woman as she got up to dispose of the potato peelings. 'I realise now that you knew and understood more than I ever gave you credit for.'

Elsie wiped her hands on a cloth and smoothed her starched white apron against her plump body before she turned back to Jo with a grave expression on her face. 'I'm glad you've come back, madam. Master Rafe was never the same after you left, and this past year...' Her words trailed off into silence and she shook her greying head as if she considered she had said too much.

'What about this past year, Elsie?' Jo prompted with an undeniable curiosity.

Elsie hesitated, clearly unsure of herself, then she moved closer to Jo and lowered her voice almost to a whisper as if she feared that she might be overheard. 'Master Rafe and Madam Averil had a terrible argument last year in April with Master Rafe's birthday,' she explained, bringing her hands together in prayer-like fashion against her ample bosom as if she was reliving that frightening experience. 'I couldn't hear what they were arguing about, but Master Rafe left Satanslaagte the next day, and Madam Averil walked around the house looking like someone who was at death's door. Master Rafe came back to the farm a week later, but he looked as if he hadn't slept or eaten for days, and ever since then he's been behaving like the devil himself.'

Jo didn't know what to make of this. She could verify the fact that there was this unfamiliar undercurrent of devilish anger in everything Rafe said or did, but she could not imagine him locked in a violent argument with his mother and, judging from what Elsie had said, it *must* have been violent.

What had caused that terrible argument? And where had Rafe rushed off to that he should have returned a week later in such a state of neglect? Jo wished she knew the answer to those questions, but she doubted that she ever would.

It was late that night, while she lay awake in bed listening to Rafe's deep, even breathing, that she remembered something else that Elsie had said.

'Master Rafe was never the same after you left.'

What could Elsie have meant by that? Jo wondered about it, but she supposed that, as with everything else, she would never know the answer.

Jo drove in to Beaufort West on the Friday afternoon to collect the pen she had had engraved with Leon Scheepers's initials. They were having dinner at the Scheepers's farm that evening, and she was not looking forward to it when she arrived back at Satanslaagte.

She had parked her Jetta in the garage beside Rafe's metallic green Mercedes and was walking towards the house when she saw a small, dusty truck parked outside the east wing of the building where the extra rooms had been added. Despite her growing curiosity she had been reluctant to intrude on the building operations during the past weeks, but this time her curiosity got the better of her, and she walked purposefully in that direction.

A young black man in a paint-stained overall was lifting one of several small, heavy-looking boxes off the back of the truck. He carried the box through the open door into the building, and Jo circled a heap of sand and gravel, taking care not to ruin the spiky heels of her shoes when she followed him inside.

The windows had been opened wide to let in air, but the smell of fresh paint filled her nostrils and caught sharply at her throat as she stood looking about her. There was a counter at the far end of the room, and beyond the counter was a smaller room with a window overlooking the koppie. Both rooms led into a passage through an arch, and Jo was about to take an involuntary step in that direction when Stan appeared in the archway.

He stopped in his tracks, visibly startled by Jo's presence, but a loud thump, followed by a muttered oath, echoed down the passage towards them, and Stan turned from Jo to cast a frowning glance in that direction.

'Hey, Piet! You be careful with those tiles, man!' He shouted his warning down the passage and received a muttered reply before he turned back to

Jo with a polite but clearly nervous, 'Good afternoon, madam.'

'Hello, Stan.' She smiled and gestured apologetically with her hands. 'I'm sorry if I startled you.'

'I didn't hear you come in, madam.'

Was that an accusation, or was he merely stating a fact? Jo wondered about this as she walked towards the wooden counter which formed a division between the two rooms and she trailed her fingers lightly over the smooth top. There was something about the layout of these rooms that disturbed her, but she could not decide what it was.

'What are these extra rooms going to be used for?' she asked, aware of Stan's dark eyes following every move she was making. When he did not answer her she turned to see him lower his gaze to the bare concrete floor and shift his weight uncomfortably from one booted foot to the other. He looked awkward and embarrassed, and suddenly Jo felt sorry for him. She was not going to have her curiosity satisfied at someone else's expense. 'I suppose I'm poking my nose into something which doesn't concern me, and if that's the case, then I won't pry.'

'This is a flat for Madam Averil,' he answered her question unexpectedly, taking out his handkerchief and wiping away the film of nervous perspiration which had gathered on his upper lip. 'She'll be moving in here when she comes back from this visit to her sister in England.'

Jo felt the shock of his statement like a blow to the forehead, and for one startled moment she reeled mentally. 'I see,' she heard herself responding, but she really didn't see at all.

Why was Averil Andersen moving out of her own home and into this small flat which Rafe had had built on to the house? Who had made this decision? Averil? Or had it been Rafe? But *why*?

She had a feeling that Stan knew the answers, but the look on his face silenced the queries that clamoured to her lips.

'Please, madam,' he begged anxiously. 'Master Rafe will kill me if he knows I told you.'

Jo did not pretend to understand the reason for this secrecy, but she was not going to add to Stan's embarrassment by insisting on an explanation. 'My lips are sealed,' she promised.

CHAPTER FIVE

JO TOOK a sip of her after-dinner liqueur and allowed her mind to wander for a moment from the conversation around her.

The dinner party at the Scheepers's farm was not the ordeal she had imagined it would be. Several other guests had been invited, many of whom Jo had not met before, but Leon and Anne Scheepers had welcomed her so warmly that the three-year lapse in her marriage to Rafe might never have occurred, and her nervousness had waned, leaving her able to cope with the few odd remarks which had come her way.

Lorin had not been as gracious as her parents. She had acknowledged Jo with a cool, disdainful nod, and after that she had ignored her while she had unashamedly monopolised Rafe's attention whenever the opportunity had presented itself.

Chris Scheepers, Lorin's brother, had arrived late for his father's birthday party. He had walked in, full of apologies, when everyone had already helped themselves to the attractively prepared buffet dinner. His gaze had swept the room to settle on Jo, and that warm smile she remembered so well had embraced her across the room. Chris had been there for her whenever she had needed a friend, and she would always be grateful to him for that.

The atmosphere at the party had been jovial from the start, but perhaps Lorin deserved a special vote of thanks for making Rafe smile more than once that evening, Jo was thinking as her glance shifted to that slender, crimson-clad figure at Rafe's side. Lorin placed a possessive hand on the sleeve of his black blazer, and she tilted her head back to look up into his face as she spoke to him. Rafe laughed at whatever it was Lorin had said to him, and Jo caught her breath on a sharp, agonising hiss which happily went unnoticed amid the clamour of voices around her.

She had caught a glimpse of the old Rafe in that laugh which Lorin had drawn from him. In that brief moment Jo had seen again the man she had fallen so madly in love with almost four years ago, and her longing for that warm, caring man was suddenly so intense that it aroused a stabbing ache in the very core of her being.

Jo felt a little faint as she picked up her glass of liqueur and excused herself from the party of women clustered together in the corner of the living-room. She needed some air, but a hand gripped her arm before she could leave the room, and she turned, smiling when she found herself looking up into Chris Scheepers's laughing blue eyes.

'I've been wanting to have a few words alone with you all evening,' he was saying as he drew her aside and urged her down on to the window-seat where she could feel the benefit of the cold night air on her hot cheeks. 'It's good to see you again, Jo, and welcome back.'

'Thank you, Chris.'

She arranged the flaring skirt of her silver-grey evening dress about her legs to make room for him on the window-seat, and he studied her intently as he sat down beside her. 'You're still one of the most beautiful women I've ever met,' he said at length, 'and I think I'm going to fall in love with you all over again.'

Jo stared at him in startled, contemplative silence, then her soft mouth quirked with amusement. 'I think you're flirting with me, Chris.'

'And why shouldn't I flirt with you?' His smile was roguish. 'It would be interesting to see if Rafe is still capable of feeling something as human as jealousy.'

She wanted to laugh, but she hastily suppressed the desire. 'What makes you think he isn't human?'

'Rafe hasn't been behaving that way for a long time, but perhaps he'll change now that you've come back into his life.'

Jo did not know what to say. What *could* she say without making Chris realise that things were not as they should be between Rafe and herself?

At the far end of the room Lorin was sliding her hands up the front of Rafe's jacket, and her fingers tugged slightly at the lapels as she raised her face to his in a gesture which was clearly an invitation to be kissed.

'There are times when I could cheerfully throttle that little sister of mine!'

Chris's vehement statement made Jo drag her gaze away from that scene playing itself out across the room. 'Don't be too harsh on your sister, Chris,' she said. 'She's in love with Rafe.'

'You *know* that?'

A mirthless smile plucked at her soft mouth as she looked into his startled eyes. 'I've always known.'

'Lorin needs a good kick in the butt!' he expounded in a savage hiss through his teeth.

'I might just do that some day,' she promised, her smile deepening.

Thank God she still had a sense of humour!

Leon Scheepers chose that moment to appear in the doorway of the crowded living-room, and he gestured anxiously to Chris. Chris cast an apologetic glance at Jo as he rose and went to his father, but some sixth sense made Jo get up and follow the two men into the hallway.

'What's the matter, Dad?' demanded Chris.

'There's been an accident,' his father explained with a look of deep concern. 'Eric was apparently hanging curtains for his wife when the ladder slipped, and I believe he fell through the lounge window.'

'You stay here, Dad,' instructed Chris. 'Let me handle this.'

Jo hastily disposed of her glass and followed Chris at a running pace into the kitchen, where she saw him haul a first-aid box out of a cupboard. 'I'd like to help, if I may,' she offered when Chris straightened. He seemed to hesitate, and she added hastily, 'Have you forgotten that I'm a qualified nurse?'

'I don't like the idea of taking you away from the party, but I think I'm going to need your nursing expertise in this instance,' he confessed, taking a bunch of keys off a hook against the wall and ushering her out of the kitchen door. 'My Land Rover is parked here at the back.'

Jo could feel the cold penetrate bitingly through her long-sleeved dress as they sped along the uneven farm track, but she forgot about her personal discomfort some minutes later when Chris brought his Land Rover to a gravel-crunching halt at the entrance to one of the cottages, where an anxious crowd had already gathered.

All that remained of the large window-pane was the few vicious-looking pieces of glass that still jutted from the frame. The rest of the glass window-pane lay scattered across a flower-bed and a section of the lawn, Jo noticed as she followed Chris into the cottage.

They followed the sound of voices coming from the kitchen, and there they found an ashen-faced black man lying on a mattress on the floor with a group of well-meaning friends hovering about him.

The group quickly dispersed when they saw Chris and Jo. Only the woman kneeling on the floor beside Eric remained, and it was obvious to Jo that she was the injured man's wife.

'I thank the lord you've come, Master Chris!' the woman exclaimed with a hint of growing hysteria in her voice. 'We carried him in here on the mattress, but we can't stop the bleeding, and I just don't know what to do any more!'

The man was shaking and in obvious shock when Jo and Chris kneeled on either side of him, and Jo left Chris to see to the first-aid box while she removed the blood-soaked towels to carry out a hasty examination.

Eric had sustained several minor cuts and abrasions, but the wounds that concerned Jo were the long gash in his left arm, and the longer, deeper gash in his right thigh where they had sensibly cut away the one leg of his trousers. The blood was pumping freely from both wounds, and that meant only one thing: severed arteries!

'He's lost too much blood already, and if we don't work swiftly he's going to lose a lot more,' Jo announced in a voice that was clipped with urgency, and she wasted no time in taking charge of the situation when she noticed that Chris had gone a sickly grey at the sight of so much blood.

'He's going to be all right, isn't he, madam?' Eric's wife demanded through her tears as she recognised the fact that Jo was experienced in these matters.

'Yes, of course,' Jo assured the woman with a practised calm, the fingers of her right hand already applying a firm pressure to the brachial artery along the inner side of Eric's upper arm while with her left hand she was guiding Chris's fingers towards the femoral artery in the man's groin. 'Apply as much pressure as you can,' she instructed him and, looking up, she saw a grim-faced Rafe entering the kitchen. She didn't have time to wonder at the reason for his presence—she was simply glad that he was there. 'We need more light, Rafe.'

He turned towards the light which hung low from the ceiling in the centre of the room, and tilted the shade so that the light shone directly on to the man who lay groaning in a semi-conscious state on the floor. He held the light steady, and while he did so he chatted calmly and reassuringly to the distraught woman, drawing her attention away from Jo's and Chris's efforts to stem the flow of blood and cover the wounds.

Jo worked as quickly as she could, but she found it difficult to hide her concern when she had secured the final tourniquet. 'You'll have to get this man to the hospital as quickly as possible, Chris,' she warned as she rose from her kneeling position to wash her hands in the kitchen sink.

She didn't have to say more. Rafe and Chris understood the urgency, and they wasted very little time in lifting Eric between them and carrying him out to the Land Rover.

Chris made sure that the semi-conscious Eric and his anxious wife were comfortably ensconced in the back of the Land Rover before he got into the driver's seat. 'Thanks, Jo,' he said, leaning out of the window. 'I don't know what I'd have done without you.'

'Get going,' she urged quietly but urgently, and moments later she was watching the Land Rover's tail-lights growing smaller down the track.

The curious crowd outside the house began to disperse, and Jo shivered, realising for the first time how cold she was, as Rafe guided her to where he had parked his Mercedes.

'You'd better have this,' said Rafe, taking off his blazer and draping it about her shoulders.

'Thanks,' she muttered, relishing the warmth of his body which still clung to the inside of the blazer, and hugging it about herself when he helped her into the car.

Was he angry with her? she wondered, slanting a quick glance at his stern profile in the light of the dashboard as he got in beside her and started the car. Should she apologise for rushing away from the party without telling him?

The words 'I'm sorry' hovered precariously on her lips, but then she remembered his insistence that, apart from sharing the same bed, they were not to intrude on each other's lives.

Dear God, how she hated this marriage that wasn't a marriage! She hated being so close to Rafe physically, and yet so far away from him emotionally that they might just as well be living on opposite sides of the earth! She wished she didn't still love him so much! She wished . . .!

Jo reined in her thoughts. If she carried on like this she would end up wallowing in self-pity, and that was the last thing she wanted.

The party was still in progress when Rafe parked his Mercedes at the gabled entrance to the homestead, and Jo was leaning forward in her seat to take off Rafe's blazer when he snapped on the interior light and turned in his seat to face her.

'You've got blood on your dress,' he said, his glance flicking over her.

'I know.' She drew the clean folds of the skirt over the soiled section to conceal the stains. 'The blood will wash out, but I can't go back into the house looking like this.'

His expression softened. No, she must have imagined it in the dim interior of the car. The eyes were too cold, the mouth too tight, and the jaw too rigid with that controlled anger she always sensed in him.

'I'll fetch your coat and your bag,' he said curtly, taking his blazer from her as he got out the car and shrugging himself into it while he strode up the steps and into the house.

Jo leaned back in her seat while she waited for him, and stared blindly up at the stars flickering in the night sky. Why was there so much anger in Rafe? Would they ever be able to speak to each other again without that undercurrent of barely controlled anger dominating their conversation?

Jo was sitting at the dressing table brushing her hair before going to bed, and Rafe had only just emerged from the shower, when she heard the telephone ringing in the hall.

'I'll get it,' she said, putting down her brush and getting to her feet.

She left the room hurriedly and quickened her pace almost to a run in the passage. She had a feeling that it would be Chris, and she was right.

'I called home first and my father told me you'd left,' he said. 'I thought you might want to know that Eric has just come out of the theatre, and the doctor says he ought to be fine after a couple of days in hospital.'

'I'm glad.' The words came out on a sigh of relief. 'I was rather worried, so I appreciate this call.'

'I'm sorry the evening had to end so early for you.'

'That doesn't matter.'

There was a brief silence before Chris asked, 'Was Rafe angry with you for rushing away from the party with me?'

'No.'

'Wasn't he even a little bit jealous?'

'Not even a little bit.' If only Rafe *had* been a little jealous then it might have given her some hope that . . .

'I suppose he must think I'm harmless,' said Chris, laughingly interrupting her thoughts. 'But little does he know,' he added, lowering his voice playfully to an animal-like growl, 'there's a beast lurking inside me that rises to the surface whenever I'm with you.'

'Don't be silly, Chris,' she rebuked him humorously, 'and goodnight.'

'Sweet dreams, sweetheart.'

The line went dead, and Jo was still smiling when she replaced the receiver, but she could feel the smile freezing on her lips as she turned and looked up to see Rafe observing her from across the hall. His big hands were thrust deep into the pockets of the green towelling robe that left his muscular legs bare from the knees down, and there was something in his narrowed, stabbing glance that was beginning to fill her with a new uneasiness.

'That was Chris,' she said, and a twisted, faintly cynical smile curved Rafe's sensuous mouth.

'So I gathered.'

'He phoned to let me know that Eric is going to be all right,' she explained, forcing herself to remain calm as she switched off the light in the hall and preceded Rafe down the passage to their room.

'I couldn't help noticing that you were getting pretty friendly with Chris after dinner this evening.'

Jo was beginning to sense the danger, and she quivered inwardly when Rafe followed her into their bedroom, but she was not going to be intimidated by him. 'If I was behaving in a friendly manner towards Chris, then it's because he *is* a friend. I always used to find him pleasant to talk to, and I still do.'

Strong fingers snaked about her arm, biting painfully into the soft flesh above her elbow, and Rafe's expression was dark and ominous as he spun her round to face him. 'Chris was flirting with you this evening, and I didn't see you make an effort to discourage him.'

'Lorin was pawing at you all evening, and I didn't see *you* discouraging *her*!' she retaliated in a sudden fury, her eyes sparking green fire as she wrenched her arm free of his clasp.

'Were you jealous?' he mocked her unexpectedly, and Jo could joyfully have slapped that hateful smile off his face, but she firmly curbed the desire.

'This conversation is bordering on the ridiculous,' she retorted stiffly, turning towards the dressing-table and brushing her hair vigorously in an attempt to work off some of her anger. 'I thought we'd agreed that our marriage was of such a nature that we were free to live our lives separate from one another?'

'You're still my wife.' His voice was a low, ominous growl. 'And I won't have you embarrassing me in public by encouraging other men to flirt with you.'

'I was *not* encouraging Chris to flirt with me—and even if I were, it's none of your business!'

'I'm *making* it my business!' he snarled, his lips drawn back against his strong white teeth as he wrenched the brush from her fingers and flung it across the room so that it landed with a thud on the carpeted floor in the corner. Jo had never seen him like this before, and the sheer savagery of his appearance made icy fear clutch at her heart. 'Do you hear me, Jo? I'm *making* it my business!'

'You can't do that, Rafe,' she pointed out with an admirable calmness into the explosive atmosphere. 'If you claim the right to query my actions, then I have just as much right to query yours, and that would put an end to the freedom you've enjoyed so much these past three years.'

She had not intended that as a barb, but it seemed to strike home with a precision that made Rafe whiten about the mouth.

'My God!' he roared suddenly, towering over her with a wild fury blazing in his eyes. 'I could——'

He broke off abruptly, and this time it was Jo who paled. Rafe had raised his hands as if to throttle her, but the next instant he turned on his heel and stormed out of the room, slamming the door behind him.

What was the matter with Rafe? Why had he been so angry? He had made the rules, so why should he be upset when she was simply acting accordingly?

Jo was suddenly shaking so much that her legs only barely managed to carry her to the bed, and she flung herself across it to bury her face in the pillow with a strangled sob on her lips.

She sat up abruptly a second later and brushed the heavy strands of hair away from her face. I'm *damned* if I'm going to cry! she reasoned with herself in silence. I've shed enough tears in this room to last me a lifetime, and I'm not going to start again now!

She drew a deep, audible breath, then released it slowly through her parted lips, and the action calmed the tremors that were still racing through her body.

Rafe had behaved like a jealous husband. But that was absurd! All he wanted from her was a legitimate heir for Satanslaagte in exchange for the loan he had given Danny, but her friendship with Chris had obviously upset him. Was it possible that he . . . ?

Jo got into bed and snapped off her thoughts along with the lights. She curled herself up into the foetal position and tried to go to sleep, but the bed felt cold and lonely without Rafe.

She was still awake an hour later when Rafe entered the bedroom. He came in quietly and got into bed beside her without switching on the light. The smell of pipe tobacco mingled with the clean, musky odour of his body, and she tensed. If he touched her now he would know she was awake. Perhaps he had already heard her heart thudding heavily against her ribs. She lay rigidly quiet, hardly daring to breathe, but she had been unnecessarily afraid.

Rafe stayed on his side of the bed. He lay with his back turned towards her, and soon his deep, even breathing told her that he was asleep.

It took a while longer for Jo to fall asleep, and she was sleeping soundly when, for the first time in weeks, that old dream returned to haunt her.

She was running up those familiar steps, but in her dream her movements were retarded and the stairs seemed endless before she entered Tony Ribeiro's flat. He was sitting at his instrument-cluttered work-bench when she burst through the door, and he was running his hands lovingly over a half-finished guitar, then he turned to her and smiled.

'Will you help me, Jo?'

'You know I'll help you, Tony. You know I will.'

The smile on his handsome face made way for a look of terrible anxiety, and he held out his hands, groping for hers, but something held her back, preventing the fingers of her outstretched hands from touching his.

'It's useless, Jo. I can't go on.'

'You can, Tony! You can!' she insisted, lunging towards his hands, but they were no longer there, and she broke out in a cold sweat at the swiftness with which the scene changed before her.

Tony was pointing the muzzle of a gun at his temple, and there was a silent accusation in his eyes which she could not understand as she watched him curl his finger about the trigger.

Suddenly there was a horrifyingly bizarre twist in the familiar nightmare. The man seated in the wheelchair was no longer Tony. It was *Rafe* who was looking at her with those dark, accusing eyes, and before she could do anything to stop him his finger had squeezed the trigger. Blood spurted from the gaping wound in his head, and a demented scream tore along Jo's throat.

The scream was still spilling from her lips when she awoke with a start to find that she was sitting bolt upright in bed. Rafe had also shot up in bed beside her, and her breath was coming in anguished, gasping sobs along her raw throat when he snapped on the bedside light.

Jo felt totally disorientated. The nightmare and the reality were still one as she sat blinking into the light. Her heart was behaving so oddly it felt as if she had a wild beast caged in her breast, and she was convinced that her saliva glands had dried up completely to leave her tongue clinging to the roof of her mouth. She stared at Rafe. Was he real, or was he a ghost?

Rafe took only one look at the dark terror in her eyes before he pulled her into his arms. 'It's all right, Jo. It's all right,' he murmured reassuringly, brushing the damp tendrils of hair away from her pale, quivering face and drawing her down under the duvet to curve her trembling body into his. 'It was only a dream.'

Only a dream! The arms that held her were very real, and so was that hard, muscular body against her own. Oh, thank God, it was only a dream!

Her shoulders started to shake and, not caring what he might think of her, she clung to him a little frantically as she gave way to those terrible, choking tears of relief which were erupting from deep within her.

Rafe slid his hand into her hair, and with his fingers gently cupping the base of her skull he pressed her head into the comforting hollow of his shoulder. 'It's all right, Jo,' he said again in that low, reassuring voice. 'Don't hold back the tears. Let them out.'

He held her as if he were comforting a child, his stroking touch soothing and calming her until her weeping ceased and she relaxed against him with a shuddering sigh on her lips.

'Feeling better?' he asked at length, combing his fingers gently through the long strands of silky auburn hair that trailed down to below her shoulders.

'Yes, thank you,' she murmured huskily against his strong, sun-browned throat.

A few hours ago Rafe had been so angry with her she had almost feared he might want to kill her, but now he was being so incredibly kind and gentle that she was reluctant to speak for fear of breaking the spell.

'I didn't think you meant it quite so literally when you said you still have nightmares about that paraplegic friend of yours.' He lifted his head off the pillow and pried her tear-stained face out into the open with his fingers beneath her chin. 'You were dreaming about him, weren't you?' he asked, his dark gaze probing hers.

'Yes,' she croaked. And no, she could have added, a haunted look entering her eyes while she tried to thrust from her mind the terrifying twist in the ending to that familiar nightmare.

'Do you want to talk about it?'

'No,' she croaked again, shrinking inwardly from the mere idea and turning her face back into the comforting hollow of his shoulder. 'Not now.'

'Shall I get you something to drink? A glass of warm milk might help you to sleep again.'

Jo moved her head in a negative reply against his warm shoulder. 'I don't want anything, thank you.'

All she needed was to soak up the living warmth of his body, and drinking in the knowledge that he was alive was the only way she could shut out the horrifying memory of that dream that lingered so persistently in her mind.

Rafe switched off the bedside light, plunging the room into darkness, but the darkness did not disturb Jo. She felt safe and secure in Rafe's arms with the length of his hard body against her own and the steady, reassuring beat of his heart beneath her ear.

His hand left her hair eventually to trail down her back, and the firm, rhythmic movement of his fingers along the hollow of her spine eased the last fragments of tension from her body.

Jo sighed deeply, relaxing at last in mind as well as body, and she stirred appreciatively against Rafe, her limbs entwining themselves with his in an unconsciously seductive way. She wanted to thank him, but she was not sure how until she felt his growing arousal against her abdomen.

Rafe groaned softly into the startled stillness between them and made to move away from her, but Jo slid her hand down his side to his firm buttock and held him there. He drew an audible breath, understanding at once what she was offering, and then his mouth was seeking hers in the darkness with a hunger to which she responded without reserve.

They kissed deeply and passionately, their tongues meeting and retreating in an erotic ritual that tantalised their senses and heightened their excitement until they were both driven to a peak of wanting more.

Rafe helped her out of her nightdress and flung the flimsy garment to the floor. Now there would be nothing between them, they would be flesh against flesh, and Rafe gathered her in to him with a low, animal-like growl on his lips.

Jo was as hungry for him as he was for her, and she revelled in the feel of those hard, rippling muscles beneath her palms when she moved her hands up across his broad back. She stroked his smooth shoulders, and threaded her fingers through his hair to guide his warm, sensuous mouth down to her breasts where his fingers had already teased her nipples into taut, aching nodules of desire.

Her mind was being stripped systematically of everything except the taste, the smell and the feel of Rafe. He knew exactly how to pleasure her body, and the probing intimacy of his stroking fingers heightened her excitement almost to the point of madness. Jo writhed beneath him, her body consumed with a desperate need for the closeness of his possession, but for some obscure reason Rafe was holding himself in check.

'Show me you want me, Jo!' he groaned against her mouth, his voice angry and impatient as he explained the reason for his odd reluctance to take her. 'Touch me, for God's sake, and show me you want me!'

Jo had been the reserved partner in their love-making sessions during these past weeks, but she discarded that reserve now to please Rafe as he had been pleasing her. She slid her hand down along his taut, flat stomach until her stroking fingers encountered his throbbing manhood, and she felt him shudder as he moaned his pleasure into her hair.

It gave her a strange sense of power to feel Rafe's magnificent body trembling beneath her gentle, manipulative hand, but it also heightened her own excitement, and she was more than ready for him when he finally entered her with a savage thrust of his hips.

Their bodies were fused together in passion and moving in perfect, rhythmic unison in their demand for satisfaction. Their senses had been honed to a sweet sharpness, spiralling them higher and higher until they spun out of control and came together in a shattering climax that left them both sated and gasping for breath.

Jo felt content for the first time in the aftermath of their lovemaking as she lay in Rafe's arms and listened to their heartbeats subsiding to a more normal pace. Her mind had wandered happily back into the past, to that time when she had believed that Rafe loved her, and she clung to that memory now, wanting desperately to believe it even if it was just for the few hours left before dawn.

'Well, that was quite a revelation,' murmured Rafe. 'If in the aftermath of your dreams you can be aroused to such phenomenal heights of passion, then perhaps you should have these nightmares more often!'

Jo rolled away from him, and she could feel her cheeks stinging with embarrassment as she sat up in bed and dragged the duvet about her. She had never felt quite so vulnerable before, and that undertone of mockery in his voice had hit her on the raw with a sickening clarity.

Nothing had changed. For the sake of her family she had allowed herself to be bought and used. There was no room for any of the finer emotions in this marriage arrangement, and she was never going to allow herself to forget that again.

She leapt out of bed without switching on the light and scooped her nightdress up off the floor. 'You're an insensitive swine, Rafe!' she hissed fiercely, resorting to anger to assuage the pain of disappointment. 'And I despise myself for thinking you could be anything else!'

Rafe seemed to find that amusing, and his mocking laughter followed her as she fled into the bathroom, where she could give vent to her shame and frustration by shedding a few tears in private.

She felt emotionally bruised deep down into her soul. How *could* she have allowed herself to believe, even for one moment, that he cared?

CHAPTER SIX

CLOUDS drifted like small tufts of white cotton wool across the blue sky, and it had become so hot in the sun that Jo had taken off her knitted jacket before descending the koppie with Fritz running at her heels.

Taking a brisk walk up on to the koppie in the mornings after an early breakfast had become a daily ritual which she rarely missed, but on this particular morning she had lingered up there on the hill for almost two hours.

She had lost track of time, thinking about her family and wondering why she had not heard from them. She had written every week since her arrival at Satanslaagte, but to date she had received nothing in return. Didn't they realise that she would be anxious to know whether everything had worked out as they had hoped?

'I've taken a tray of tea through to the lounge, and you have a visitor, madam,' Elsie announced all in one breath when the screen door into the kitchen slammed shut behind Jo.

'Who is it?' Jo asked cautiously.

'It's Master Chris, madam.'

This was unexpected, and unusual. Chris Scheepers had never made a habit of dropping in uninvited at Satanslaagte.

'Thank you, Elsie,' Jo murmured thoughtfully, walking on through the kitchen and down the passage into the hall.

Chris had been standing at the window, looking out across the garden, but he turned when he heard Jo entering the living-room and flashed that boyish smile she remembered so well.

Her frown faded and her mouth curved in an answering smile. 'I hope you haven't been waiting long?'

'I'd wait a lifetime for you, Jo,' he said, taking the hand she had offered him and raising it to his lips.

'Don't say things like that,' she rebuked him gently, gesturing him into an armchair when he released her fingers. 'I know you're not serious, but remarks like that can so very easily be misinterpreted.'

'It never used to bother you before,' he pointed out, eyeing her speculatively when they sat facing each other across the low, marble-topped table where Elsie had placed the tray of tea and scones.

'Things are different now,' she said without thinking, and she could have kicked herself the next instant when she saw his glance sharpen with interest.

'How different?'

Jo looked away and changed the subject. 'We'd better have our tea and eat the scones while they're still fresh.'

She felt his curious glance resting on her during the ensuing silence while she poured their tea and offered him a scone, and she had an uneasy feeling that he was not going to leave the matter there.

'You haven't answered my question, Jo,' he prompted, confirming what she had suspected when they settled back in their chairs with their tea. 'What's so different about your marriage this time around?'

'I don't want to talk about it.'

'Why not?'

'I've said too much already, Chris,' she brushed aside his query. 'It was a slip of the tongue, and I regret it, so let's just leave it at that.'

His speculative gaze held hers for seemingly endless seconds, then he nodded. 'I won't pry, Jo, but I'll always be here for you if you should need someone to talk to.'

'I know... and I thank you for that.' She took a sip of tea and felt the tension ease slowly out of her body. 'You haven't told me yet to what I owe the pleasure of your company this morning.'

'I was on my way home from the hospital when I decided to drop in.'

'There's nothing wrong, is there?' The clinical side of Jo was instantly on the alert. 'Eric hasn't had a relapse, has he?'

Chris shook his head reassuringly. 'The patient is healing nicely, and the doctor says he should be able to come home tomorrow.'

'That's wonderful!' she exclaimed in relief.

He held her glance, his expression grave. 'Eric has you to thank for his quick recovery, and we're all in your debt.'

His praise embarrassed her. She had done no more than anyone else with a good knowledge of first aid would have done, and she did not want anyone to feel indebted to her for being on hand to help.

'Have another scone,' she suggested, offering Chris the plate.

'Are you trying to *shut* me up, or *fatten* me up?' he demanded, his smile teasing as he helped himself to a buttered scone and bit into it.

'Both,' she confessed, flicking a faintly critical glance over his lean, long-limbed body ensconced in the chair facing hers. 'I couldn't help noticing the other night that you've lost a lot of weight in the three years since I last saw you. Have you been ill?'

Jo's innocent observation triggered off an unexpected and startling reaction. Chris's eyes darkened with pain, and for one awful moment she thought he was going to cry, but he seemed to pull himself together as he rose abruptly and walked to the window. He stood with his back to her, his hands pushed into the pockets of his brown corded trousers and his shoulders hunched beneath his tweed jacket.

She had unintentionally touched him on the raw, and she was still wondering what she could say or do to rectify the situation when Chris surprised her by launching into an explanation.

'I met a girl last year. Alice Montgomery,' he said, his voice clipped and his sentences disjointed with the obvious effort to remain in control of himself. 'We were going to be married. She was driving home to George to spend Christmas with her parents.' His shoulders moved beneath his jacket as if he was making a physical attempt to ward off the pain of remembering. 'There was an accident.'

Compassion tugged painfully at Jo's heart. 'Was she killed?'

'Oh, God, if only she *had* been killed, then it might have been easier for me!' His voice cracked with emotion, and he took a moment to pull himself together before he turned to face Jo. 'She's been in a coma ever since the accident,' he gestured helplessly with his hands, 'and the chances are slim that she'll ever come out of it.'

His anguished expression drew Jo to her feet. 'I'm so sorry, Chris,' she murmured sympathetically, going to him, and taking his hands in her own.

He lowered his gaze to those small, capable hands gripping his and a crooked, faintly embarrassed smile curved his mouth. 'I guess we all have our problems, and I certainly didn't come here today with the intention of burdening you with mine.'

'I'm glad you told me,' she assured him with a quiet sincerity as she urged him back into his chair and poured him another cup of tea.

Half an hour later when Chris left, his deep sorrow was carefully tucked away behind his boyishly charming smile, but Jo's heart bled for him. She had worked too long in a hospital not to know of the pain and suffering endured by the family and friends of a comatose patient, and she could only pray that in this instance the agony would not be prolonged.

Talking with Chris had made her forget her own problems, but at the end of that week, when there was still no news from Cape Town, she decided to phone her mother. She dialled the home number, and the telephone seemed to ring for interminable seconds before it was answered.

'Harris residence. Lavinia Harris speaking.'

'Hello, Mother.'

'Jo? Is that you, Jo?' came the somewhat startled query.

'As far as I know I'm your only daughter, so who else would be calling you "Mother"?' Jo demanded sharply and with an unaccustomed ring of sarcasm in her voice.

'Are you all right, Jo?'

'Of *course* I'm all right,' she brushed her mother's anxious query aside with a measure of impatience. 'How are things at home? What's going on? I've written every week, but you haven't answered my letters. You did get my letters, didn't you?'

'Yes, yes, I received your letters, and I've been wanting to write, Jo, but I—er—I haven't really had time.'

That odd hesitation in Lavinia's voice alerted Jo to something which she could not define at that moment. 'Did everything work out all right for Danny?' she persisted. 'Is everything settled with the business?'

'Yes, I—er—yes, everything is . . . just fine.'

'You don't sound very sure,' Jo accused suspiciously.

'Of *course* I'm sure,' Lavinia insisted in much stronger tones. 'You know I've never had much to do with the business, but Danny assures me that everything is going well.'

'Good!' Jo sighed audibly. 'I'm glad.'

Lavinia was by nature an extremely talkative person, but on this occasion she was oddly reticent, and Jo was frowning down at the black and white tiled floor in the hall when their conversation ended moments later. She had hoped that speaking to her mother would ease her mind, but instead it did exactly the reverse.

Was there something the matter, or was she imagining it? Danny would know, she decided, lifting the receiver again and dialling her brother's private number at the office.

Danny's secretary answered the phone and, recognising Jo's voice, she put her through to Danny without delay.

'Hello? Jo?' Danny's voice was clearly agitated when it came on the line. 'Are you all right?'

'That was the first question Mother asked me,' Jo responded testily. 'For goodness' sake, Danny, why *shouldn't* I be all right?'

The line crackled with silence for a second or two. 'You've spoken to Mother?' asked Danny.

'A moment ago, yes. She sounded strangely distracted. Do you know that I actually got the feeling she didn't want to talk to me?'

Danny laughed unexpectedly. 'I'm sure you're just imagining things, Jo.'

'Perhaps I am,' she agreed with him, but she was not entirely convinced. 'You're not hiding something from me, are you? Mother isn't ill or something, is she?'

'I assure you Mother was in perfect health when I left the house this morning. Look, Jo, I must rush,' he added abruptly. 'I've got someone waiting to see me. Give my best to Rafe, will you?'

'Yes, sure I'll——' She stopped in mid-sentence when she realised that the connection had already been severed, and she felt strangely isolated as she dropped the lifeless receiver back on to its cradle.

Why did she have the feeling that neither her mother nor Danny had wanted to talk to her? Was it her imagination, or had they actually sounded nervous?

That long list of questions in her mind was getting longer instead of shorter. She needed some answers, but she wasn't getting any, and if she didn't get out of the house for a while she would go crazy with frustration.

Jo went for a brisk walk to clear her head, but she was passing the old store-room below the stables when she stopped suddenly to stare contemplatively at the thatch-roofed building.

She had passed the store-room every day on her way up to the koppie, but this time she walked purposefully towards it. The paint was peeling badly on the wooden door and she wondered if the rusted bolt still worked. It did, but the hinges on the door squealed in protest when she pushed it open, and the dusty, musty smell made her wrinkle her nose when she stepped inside.

The store-room was littered with large, empty crates and cardboard boxes, and rusted iron standards lay scattered on the floor against the far wall. The remaining space was cluttered with broken, antiquated farming equipment, and everything was coated in a thick layer of dust.

It was a big room, big enough to accommodate at least twenty people, and an idea took shape in her mind as she stood looking about her. This would be an ideal place to meet with the women who attended the twice-weekly homecraft classes.

Jo was jolted out of her contemplative stance moments later when a mouse darted past her feet, and she leapt aside, dislodging a cardboard box with her flailing arm. It tumbled to the concrete floor, taking several smaller boxes with it, and in the process it also stirred up a cloud of dust that billowed wildly in the shaft of afternoon sunlight which entered the store-room through the old sash windows.

The dormant layer of dust had already irritated her sensitive nostrils, but, set in motion, it started a riot in her nasal passages. Jo sneezed ... and sneezed again. She had to get out of the store-room, she was thinking as she sneezed repeatedly into her lacy handkerchief. She turned, and had barely taken a pace in the direction of the door when the gritty sound of a heavy boot on the sandy floor made her look up sharply to see Rafe's massive, khaki-clad frame blocking the exit.

Her heart leapt nervously into her throat and seemed to remain there. Was she trespassing?

'Looking for something?' he asked when she stopped sneezing, and she could not tell whether he was angry with her for being there, or merely curious.

'No, I—I was just wondering——'

'You were wondering?' he prompted when she halted with uncertainty.

Jo blew her nose and wiped the tears out of her eyes to give herself time to think. Should I risk it? Should I ask him? Oh, what the hell! 'I was wondering if this store-room was being used for anything in particular?'

'As you can see——' with a sweeping gesture of his hand he encompassed the entire room and its contents '—it's being used mainly for hoarding rubbish. Why do you ask?'

'The group of women attending the homecraft classes has grown to such an extent that we're in desperate need of a place to work, and this store-room would be ideal if—if you would allow me the use of it.'

Her words seemed to hang heavily in the dusty air between them as they stood facing each other, and Jo held her breath when Rafe finally averted his narrowed, probing glance to survey the room. His mouth had tightened and, watching him, she saw his strong jaw harden. Was he going to refuse?

'A couple of beams need to be reinforced, some of the window-panes will have to be replaced, and the walls and woodwork could do with a coat of paint.' His eyes met hers as he delivered his verdict. 'It may take a week before it will be ready for you to move in.'

Jo felt a little giddy with relief and excitement. 'That would be perfect.'

'I'll make the necessary arrangements first thing in the morning,' he said, turning to leave.

'Rafe!' Her hand on his arm stopped him before he could step out of the door, and she reached up impulsively, drawing his head down to hers to kiss him on the lips. 'Thank you.'

Rafe stared at her, his neck and shoulders taut beneath her hands and his features impassive except for the visible tightening of the muscles along the side of his jaw. 'Do you miss living in the city?'

The question was as unexpected as his cool response to her kiss, and she dropped her hands to her sides to take an embarrassed pace away from him. 'No, I don't miss the city,' she answered truthfully.

'What stopped you from settling down the last time?' he demanded with that underlying anger in his deep, throaty voice.

Your mother. The words spilled into her mouth, but she gulped them back forcibly because it would not have been the truth. A great deal of the blame could be laid at her own door, but this was neither the time nor the place for a full confession.

'I was younger then, and perhaps a little immature,' she replied, passing off his query with a shrug and avoiding his dark, probing gaze. 'What does it matter now?'

'Perhaps you weren't assertive enough.'

Jo had discovered that truth for herself a long time ago. She had retreated into her shell instead of fighting for her rights as Rafe's wife. Time had not eradicated the problem as she had hoped it would, and the only thing she had achieved was to drive herself into a strangulated corner of her own making.

'Would it have changed anything if I had been more assertive?' she asked, despising herself for that eternal flame of hope that burned inside her, and she had all the more reason to hate herself when his eyes flicked over her dispassionately.

'Probably not,' he concluded, ducking his head to step through the door, and then he was striding away in the direction of the stables.

Jo's heart felt heavy when she walked back to the house. After five weeks of marriage to Rafe she was still finding it difficult to adapt to the emotional see-saw her life had become. There had been times when she had felt the tension ease between them, but then, without warning, Rafe would shatter that illusion of normality in their relationship.

Why did he do it? And why did she sometimes get the feeling that the terrible anger inside him was directed at her? What had she done to deserve it?

More questions! Dear God! When was she going to get some *answers*?

The activities in and around the house kept Jo too busy during the ensuing three weeks to dwell on questions for which she could find no answers. The store-room had been cleaned out and repaired within a week, as Rafe had promised, but it took another week to move in. Jo had made the curtains, but the women had furnished the store-room themselves with odd chairs and tables which they had brought from their homes.

Jo was happy that she had this project with which to keep herself occupied, but she had already begun to look ahead. The homecraft classes would eventually peter out, and then, perhaps, the storeroom could be converted into a clinic, but that was still in the future, and Jo was not so sure that Rafe would agree.

The flat had also reached completion, with a door being broken through into the living-room. This would give Averil direct access to the house as well as a private exit into the garden.

Jo had taken the noise and the mess of the building operations in her stride, but when she had tried to question Rafe about it his features had become hard and forbidding, and she supposed she would simply have to wait until he saw fit to give her an explanation.

She also received news from her mother during this time. Lavinia Harris had written a pleasant and informative letter, but Jo could still not shake off that curious feeling that something was not as it should be. Her imagination was running riot, and she could not rein it in. Something was wrong, but for some obscure reason the truth was being hidden from her.

Jo left the house one morning to embark on her usual walk up on to the koppie, and the air was scented and warm with the first day of spring less than a week away. The bank of clouds on the horizon was heavy with the promise of rain, but sometimes, for weeks and months on end in the Karoo, that was all the clouds would be—a promise of rain lurking on the far distant horizon.

She raised her hand to shade the morning sun from her eyes as she glanced in the direction of the neighbouring property. The Scheepers's farm lay to the east of Satanslaagte, and the boundary dividing the two vast properties was situated approximately a mere hundred metres beyond the eastern slope of the koppie. Jo had not seen Lorin these past weeks, but she had bumped into Chris on one occasion when she had gone shopping in Beaufort West. They had had tea together, and Jo could remember thinking that he had become a rather gaunt replica of the man she had once known.

A movement caught Jo's eye just as she was about to turn her back on the sun and, using both her hands to shade her eyes, she stared out across the veld beyond Satanslaagte's boundary to where a clump of acacia trees grew lustrously beside a windmill in the distance.

A horse had been tethered to one of the acacia trees. It was the dapple-grey mare which Chris always favoured, and there was no mistaking the man who was sitting on the edge of the low drinking-trough beside the water tank. It was Chris.

That was odd, she thought. The camp was not being grazed, and the only reason for dismounting in that particular spot would be to repair the windmill or to check the flow of water, but Chris was doing neither.

Something was wrong!

Jo hurried down the eastern slope of the koppie with Fritz bounding down ahead of her, and she jogged the remaining hundred metres towards the boundary.

'Go home, Fritz. Go home, boy,' she instructed the Alsatian when she reached the fence. Fritz whined and dropped his tail between his hind legs, but he had been trained well, and he did as he was told. 'Good boy, Fritz,' Jo encouraged the animal on his way.

The jackal fencing was more than a metre high, and she climbed over it cautiously, taking care not to catch her denims on the cruel wire barbs. She still had a long way to go when she dropped down on the other side, at least another hundred metres or more, and she was glad that she had exercised daily when she started out across the scrub-covered earth at an easy, jogging pace.

Jo slowed down to a walking pace when she neared the windmill. Chris was still sitting on the edge of the knee-high concrete trough in the shade of the acacias. His head was bowed, his elbows rested on his khaki-sheathed thighs, and his hands hung limply between his knees. He did not hear Jo approaching, and her steps faltered when she was a few paces away from him. She felt unsure of herself, but it was too late now to wonder if she had the right to intrude.

'Chris?' She spoke his name softly, and she was shocked when he lifted his head to look at her. His jaw was unshaven, his glazed eyes were bloodshot and heavy-lidded, and he looked as if he had aged years since the last time she had seen him. 'I was up on the koppie when I saw your horse, and I realised something was wrong. What is it, Chris?'

'They called early this morning,' he said, his throat working and his eyes filling with tears. 'She's dead, Jo. Alice is dead.'

'Oh, Chris, I'm so sorry!' She went to him then, to comfort him, and she held him against her like a child with his head resting against her breast.

'Do you know that I actually prayed for this?' he told her. 'I believed I'd feel better when it was all over, but I don't.'

'It will take time,' she said quietly, stroking his hair in a soothing gesture until the silence was disturbed by a mournful squeal emanating from the windmill when the breeze drifting across the veld turned the blades.

'Oh, lord, I'm making quite a spectacle of myself, aren't I?' he groaned, relinquishing his hold on her and looking embarrassed.

'It's all right, Chris,' she responded calmly, seating herself beside him on the edge of the trough and looking away when he reached into his trouser pocket for his handkerchief. 'You're just being human,' she added reassuringly.

Chris blew his nose and wiped his eyes. It took a while for him to regain control, and his voice was reasonably steady when he finally informed her of his plans. 'I'm leaving for George this afternoon to help with the funeral arrangements,' he said.

'Are you taking anyone with you?' she asked, concerned about him driving all that way on his own and in his present emotional state.

'My mother will be accompanying me.' He pocketed his handkerchief and sighed heavily as he stared down at his dusty boots. 'You know, I've been expecting this for a long time, but it was still such a shock when it happened.'

'It always is.' She could still remember vividly what a traumatic time it had been for the family when her father had died, and, even though they had all known he would never recover from the stroke he had suffered, it had not diminished the shock of his eventual death.

'What am I going to do, Jo?'

'Take one day at a time,' she suggested quietly, 'and be grateful that it took months and not years to end everyone's suffering.'

He nodded. 'Yes, I suppose I should be grateful for that.'

The windmill squealed once again when the warm breeze shifting across the dry earth slowly turned the steel blades to pump a weak stream of water into the concrete tank behind them.

Chris got to his feet after a while and the smile curving his mouth was devoid of humour. 'I guess I can't sit here all morning when there's work to be done.'

'Keep in mind that work is an excellent therapy,' said Jo, getting up to dust the seat of her blue denims.

'You sound as if you've had experience of that.'

'I have,' she confessed with a wry smile as she walked with him to where he had tethered his horse. 'I'll be thinking of you, Chris, and I'll be praying for you.'

'Thank you, Jo. You're a good friend.' He hugged her briefly and kissed her on the cheek before he mounted the dapple-grey mare. 'Would you like a ride to the fence?'

'I'll walk, thanks,' she declined his offer, and he raised his hand in a casual salute before he rode off in the direction of the homestead.

Jo felt sad as she walked the distance back to the boundary fence and climbed over it. Life could often be cruel, and fate had somehow dealt Chris the cruellest blow.

She was skirting the koppie on her way back to the house when the pounding of a horse's hoofs on the hard earth made her stop and turn at the gate into the yard to see Rafe riding towards her from the direction of the plane trees which grew so densely further down along the boundary fence. The brim of his felt hat with the leather band was pulled down over his forehead, shading his eyes from the glare of the sun, but even at a distance Jo could see the hardness of his jaw and the thin, disapproving line of his mouth.

Fritz ran alongside the black stallion, but he darted ahead the last few paces and bounded towards Jo to greet her with an excited bark. She bent down to pat the Alsatian, but backed away a couple of nervous paces when Rafe dismounted and tethered his horse to the gatepost.

'When I saw Fritz arrive at the house without you I thought you'd fallen and injured yourself.' Rafe's dark eyes stabbed at her accusingly and there was a leashed fury in his manner when he thumbed his hat on to the back of his head. 'Now I know what these early morning walks are in aid of. It's a cover-up for your secret meetings with Chris!'

Jo couldn't decide whether to feel amused or angry, but she was more inclined to feel the latter. Rafe had been observing her from the shadows of the plane trees while she had been comforting Chris—she realised that now—and he had drawn his own conclusions from what he had seen.

'Alice Montgomery died this morning,' she said at length in a calm and admirably controlled voice, and the look on Rafe's face told her that he knew exactly whom she was speaking of. He did not deserve an explanation, Jo was thinking, but he was going to get one all the same. 'I was up on the koppie when I happened to notice Chris sitting under the acacia trees, and I wouldn't have gone to him if I hadn't suspected that something might be wrong. The news of Alice's death has upset him a great deal even though he's been expecting it, and I did what I could—as a friend—to comfort him. Wouldn't you have done the same?'

Rafe's eyes burned down into hers for a moment before he spun away from her with a savage oath on his lips. 'God knows that lately there are times when I don't know myself!'

'If that's an apology, then I accept it.'

'Just a minute, Jo,' he said, his hand on her shoulder stopping her in her tracks when she would have turned on her heel to walk away from him.

His ruggedly handsome face looked distorted through the film of angry tears which had leapt into her eyes, and she heard him mutter something unintelligible before she was caught up against his hard chest. The smell of horseflesh and sun mingled pleasantly with his particular brand of aftershave as he set his mouth on hers in a kiss that assaulted her senses, and she was shaken to the core when he finally released her to mount his horse.

'I'll see you later,' he said abruptly, and then he was gone, urging the stallion into a wild gallop across the veld with Fritz following close behind.

Jo watched him go until he was no more than a tiny moving speck in the shimmering distance, and suddenly she was smiling. Rafe was not quite as indifferent as he had wanted her to believe. He could still feel for others, and that was a warming thought which would stay with her for the rest of that day.

CHAPTER SEVEN

JO WAS in a thoughtful mood when she dropped her earrings into the porcelain bowl on the dressing-table and stepped out of the white shoes she had worn with her lilac dress that evening. She was thinking about Chris, and wondering how he would cope with his loss, when she looked up to see Rafe emerging from the dressing-room.

'My mother will be arriving home on Saturday,' he announced unexpectedly, taking off his towelling robe and getting into bed.

So soon? The words screamed through her mind on a note of panic. 'Will you be meeting her at the airport in Cape Town?'

'I'm sending Stan down to meet her.'

Now! He'll have to tell me now! Jo picked up the nightdress that lay draped across the foot of the bed and said innocently, 'I'll see to it that her room is cleaned and aired before she arrives.'

'That won't be necessary.' His eyes held hers, but his features remained inscrutable as he leaned back against the pillows and laced his fingers together behind his head. 'My mother will be staying in the flat which has been built on to the house, and her bedroom furniture, plus several other oddments from the house, will be transferred to the flat the day before she returns.'

'Why haven't you told me this before?'

'Until today there wasn't any need for you to be told,' he drawled lazily. 'It isn't any of your business, really.'

'But it *is* my business, Rafe.'

Anger propelled her towards the bed, but she found herself momentarily distracted by that aura of raw masculinity he exuded. She was staring at the wide expanse of his chest, and her eyes involuntarily trailed the narrowing V of body hair down along his taut, flat stomach to where the duvet formed a barrier across his lean hips, but then she had to take a firm grip on her flaring senses. This was her opportunity to find an answer to some of those troubling queries in her mind, and she was not going to let the moment pass.

'Why is your mother moving out of the house?' she tried again.

His face hardened in the soft glow of the bedside light. 'It's best this way.'

That didn't tell her much. 'Best for whom?' she asked.

'Best for both my mother and myself.'

'Was it a joint decision?'

'The decision was mine.'

There was something about that quietly spoken statement that made Jo realise she would be at risk if she continued to question him on this subject. Would she ever know the truth? She sighed inwardly and was about to turn away when her night-dress was snatched from her fingers without warning.

'I don't know why you bother to wear something when you ought to know by now that I'm just going to take it off again,' Rafe chided her unexpectedly, his voice deepening on a note of sensuality that made her nerve-ends tingle in response.

'I'm trying to preserve what little dignity I still have left.' She was outwardly calm despite that treacherous quickening of her pulses, and her hand was remarkably steady when she held it out for the filmy garment he was drawing idly through his fingers. 'Give me that, Rafe.'

'This flimsy thing adds mystery to your body, and part of the excitement is having to peel it off you, but it's much more exciting to watch a woman undress herself.' She should have known what to expect—it was there in the glowing depths of his dark eyes and the sensuous curve of his mouth—but it still came as a shock when he commanded softly, 'Strip for me, Jo.'

Her eyes were emerald pools of astonishment in her flushed face, and in the shadowy hollow at the base of her throat a tiny pulse was beginning to throb erratically. 'You must be mad if you think I'll stand here and——'

'Strip, Jo!' He cut across her indignant protest in an ominously soft voice, and his smile mocked and challenged her simultaneously while he bundled up her nightdress and thrust it under his pillows. 'Or would you prefer me to tear that lovely, expensive dress off your body?'

Jo did not doubt for one moment that he would do exactly as he had said, and her hand rose involuntarily—almost protectively—to the wide, delicately embroidered collar of her pale lilac dress. The dress was of the purest silk, and the price had set her back almost a month's salary, but she couldn't resist purchasing the dress when she had seen it in a shop window several months ago in Cape Town.

'You never leave me with much of a choice, do you?' she accused stiffly while her mind was searching frantically for a way out of this dilemma.

'You could always buy yourself a new dress.'

'I hate needless waste,' she protested before she could stop herself, and the glitter of triumph in Rafe's eyes made her realise that she had lost.

'In that case,' he smiled lazily, 'strip.'

Jo wished that she could shrink into the carpeted floor and remain there forever. Rafe stirred impatiently and, afraid that he might carry out his threat, she started to undo the tiny pearl buttons down the front of her dress.

His eyes were like darting flames. They leapt at every movement of her hands as she discarded her clothes, and they seemed to scorch her skin as she slowly exposed her body for his desirous inspection. His burning gaze lingered on her small, firm breasts after she had peeled off her bra, then it dipped lower to follow the last lacy garment as it slid to the floor along her shapely thighs, and it was at this point that Jo realised she was no longer embarrassed, only curiously excited as she stood naked before him.

'Come here,' he growled, flinging aside the duvet, and reaching for her impatiently.

Jo landed on top of him, flesh against flesh, and it felt as if every taut muscle in his magnificent male body was suddenly being stamped into the length of her soft, feminine frame. One hand settled on her firm bottom to grind her hips into his while the other came to rest at the nape of her neck, and they remained like that for a moment, their glances locked antagonistically, then he dragged her mouth down to his.

The white-hot passion of his kiss drew a matching response from Jo, and her body was eager for his when he eased his mouth from hers to release her hair from its confining combs. Her hair fell forward over her smooth shoulders like a golden brown veil, and her scalp tingled pleasantly when he plunged his hands into its silken thickness.

'You're so beautiful.' Flames of desire were leaping in his heavy-lidded eyes while his glance traced the delicate contours of her face. 'I can't seem to get enough of you.'

Jo wished she could think of a scathing response to that statement, but her mind refused to function normally. Her body was craving fulfilment, and for the moment that was all that mattered, she realised, as she lowered her mouth to his invitingly. His tongue slid between her parted lips to explore and draw on the sweet moistness within, and coherent thought was no longer possible when he slowly rolled her over on to her back.

They made love with a fierce urgency, their bodies straining relentlessly towards that ultimate moment of exquisite physical release. Afterwards, when they lay sated in each other's arms, Jo could barely recognise herself in the wild, wanton behaviour she had displayed during that passionate drive towards the satisfaction her body had craved.

What's happening to me? she wondered agitatedly when Rafe switched off the bedside light to plunge the room into darkness. Making love had never been this frenzied before, nor quite as desperate. Could it have something to do with the fact that Averil Andersen would be returning to Satanslaagte at the end of the week?

Jo felt her insides spasm nervously at the thought of Rafe's mother, and she untangled her limbs from his to sit up in bed. 'Rafe?' She took him by the shoulder and shook him. 'Are you awake?'

'I am now,' he muttered with a measure of annoyance in his sleep-filled voice.

'You can't move your mother out into that flat.'

'It's all settled,' he grunted, thumping his pillows into shape and turning over on to his side to lie with his back to her.

'You can't do it, Rafe!'

Silence greeted her statement, and she thought for a moment that he was going to ignore her, but then he switched on the bedside light and turned over on to his back. 'What makes you think I can't do it?' he demanded, frowning up at her.

'This has been your mother's home since before you were born, Rafe,' she argued with him. 'You can't banish her now to a few small rooms, no matter how nice and new they might be.'

'I'm not banishing my mother from the rest of the house, I'm merely giving her a place in our home where she'll have total freedom to do as she pleases.' His frown became an angry scowl. 'And may I ask what right have you to question my decision?'

'I'm not questioning your decision,' she contradicted him calmly. 'I'm trying to appeal to your better nature.'

His face hardened. 'I know what I'm doing, Joceline!'

The full use of her name acted as a warning not to pursue the matter, and when he switched off the light she slid down beneath the duvet to lie frowning into the darkness.

Rafe might have his reasons for wanting his mother to move into that flat, but to Jo it made no sense, and neither did it feel right. Averil Andersen was a proud, autocratic woman, and she had done everything within her power to maintain her hold on what she had considered *her* kingdom. What could have happened to make her give way to Rafe's decision that she should move out of her home and into the flat?

It was futile attempting to unravel the situation. The more she tried, the more entangled it became and, sighing tiredly, she closed her eyes and tried to go to sleep.

Jo had stationed herself out on the shady stoep on the Saturday afternoon. She had thought she might keep herself occupied with her crocheting, but it lay untouched in her lap while her gaze remained fixed on the road leading up to the house.

She wished Rafe would hurry the repairs to the water pump so that he could come home. The nervous anxiety which had been building up inside her all week was now fast reaching its peak. If only

Rafe would come home! She did not want to be alone when Averil Andersen arrived.

Jo picked up her crochet work in a renewed attempt to while away the time, but she lowered it to her lap again a few minutes later. How would Averil react? Would she be cool and polite, or would she be openly hostile? A moving cloud of dust caught Jo's attention and her stomach muscles seemed to spasm nauseatingly. She would soon have the answer to those queries.

She hurried into the house to inform Elsie that she could make the tea and bring the tray through to the living-room, then she went out on to the stoep again to await Averil Andersen's arrival. Where was Rafe? What could be taking him so long?

Several agonising minutes elapsed before the metallic-green Mercedes came up the drive towards the house with Averil seated comfortably in the back and Stan at the wheel acting as chauffeur.

Jo remained standing on the stoep until the vehicle was brought to a halt, and it was only when Stan walked round the bonnet of the car to open the door for Averil that Jo went down the steps to greet her mother-in-law.

Rafe, where *are* you?

Averil Andersen was tall and still remarkably slender for a woman in her late sixties, and she was expensively dressed in a long-sleeved blue dress with her favourite pearls about her throat. The short hair which was styled so elegantly about her regally held head had changed colour from streaky grey to snow-white, but other than that she still looked exactly as Jo had remembered her.

'Welcome home, Mrs Andersen.' Jo had her years of rigorous training as a nurse to thank for the outward calmness with which she looked into that haughty face on a level with her own.

There was no warmth in the dark, assessing gaze that swept up to meet hers, and Jo was beginning to think that the hand she held out in greeting was going to be ignored when she suddenly felt Averil's cool fingers clasping hers.

'You must be tired,' said Jo, taking a steadying grip on Averil's arm when she saw her swaying slightly on her feet.

'The journey by car from Cape Town has been rather tiring,' Averil admitted and, leaving Stan to see to her luggage, she allowed Jo to assist her up the steps and into the cool interior of the house.

Elsie hovered respectfully in the hall to welcome Averil home, and they exchanged a few words before Elsie returned to the kitchen, leaving Jo to usher Averil into the living-room where a tray of tea and biscuits awaited them.

Averil lowered herself into a chair with an audible sigh on her lips before she cast a brief glance about the room. Those dark, piercingly sharp eyes were so like Rafe's, and they would not have missed the few changes Jo had made in the room, but, surprisingly, she said nothing.

'Where is Rafe?' She finally asked the question which Jo had been asking herself for the past hour.

'I'm expecting him any moment now, but he said we should have our tea if he was late, and not to wait for him.' Jo had seated herself on the edge of the sofa to pour their tea, and she was relieved to see that her hand was steady when she passed Averil her cup.

Averil's taut mouth relaxed, and she smiled for the first time as she helped herself to a biscuit from the plate Jo proffered. 'I'm glad to see that Elsie remembered to bake my favourite ginger biscuits.'

'Elsie was busy this morning, so I baked them.'

The smile faded. 'I didn't know you could bake.'

There was a sting in that remark, but Jo chose to ignore it as she caught sight of Rafe through the living-room window. Thank goodness he was here!

'Hello, Mother,' he said when he entered the room, and Jo was astonished at the lack of warmth in his voice and manner.

'Rafe!'

Averil remained seated, but there was something almost pathetic in the way her face had lit up when she saw her son, and Jo felt her heart contract with compassion when Rafe leaned over his mother to kiss her briefly and coolly on the cheek.

'You're looking well, Mother,' Rafe announced with a tight smile as he seated himself on the sofa beside Jo and accepted the cup of tea she passed him in silence.

'You said I would enjoy an extended visit with my sister, and I did, but it's good to be back again on familiar soil.'

Prompted by Rafe, his mother mentioned some of the places she had visited during her stay in the British Isles, and while they talked Jo could not help but become aware of an element of strain which had not been there before between Rafe and his mother. Did this still stem from that argument they had had more than a year ago? The argument which Elsie said had taken place on Rafe's birthday the previous year?

The conversation finally petered out, and there was an awkward silence before Averil leaned forward to place her empty cup on the tray. 'Is my flat ready for me?' she asked.

'Everything is as you wanted it.' Rafe got up and held out his hand to help his mother out of her chair. 'Let me show you.'

Jo had also risen, but Rafe indicated with a brief gesture of his hand that she should remain in the living-room, and she nodded acceptance. She had dreaded this moment, and she was relieved that Rafe had considered it unnecessary for her to accompany them.

She waited until the inter-leading door closed behind Rafe and his mother before she turned towards the window and stared thoughtfully out across the spacious garden where the late afternoon sun was casting long shadows across the neatly trimmed lawn.

Meeting Averil again after all these years had not been as difficult as she had imagined it might be. She was not quite sure what she had expected, but she had certainly not imagined she would be meeting a subdued version of the woman she had once known.

Subdued? Yes, that was where the difference lay in the relationship between Rafe and his mother. A cataclysmic change had occurred to place Rafe in command as master of his home as much as he was master of his land, and Averil had become subdued in the process of relinquishing control over her portion of that kingdom.

Jo heard the door open and close behind her and she turned to see Rafe walking towards her. 'Is everything all right?' she asked, meeting him halfway across the carpeted floor.

'Mother is going to unpack her suitcases, and then she'll most probably rest a while before dinner.' His smile mocked her. 'What were you so worried about?'

'I wasn't worried,' she lied.

Rafe cupped her chin in his hand, tilting her face up to his and forcing her to meet his eyes while he brushed his thumb in a light caress across her bottom lip. 'I don't know if you're aware of it, but there's a little nerve at the corner of your mouth that tends to jump whenever you're nervous or agitated, and it's been jumping all day.'

'I don't like the idea that your mother has moved out of her own home,' Jo confessed reluctantly against that tantalising thumb. 'I can't help feeling guilty about it.'

His face hardened and his hand dropped to his side. 'You have absolutely nothing to feel guilty about.' He turned towards the fireplace and selected a pipe off the rack on the mantelshelf. 'This was my suggestion, and Mother agreed to it without hesitation.'

'*Was* it simply a suggestion, or was it a decision that left your mother without a choice?' she asked suspiciously, well aware of his ability to manoeuvre someone into a position which was devoid of options.

'It was a suggestion which she could have turned down if she'd wanted to.'

Jo tried to gauge Rafe's thoughts while he fingered tobacco into the bowl of his pipe and struck a match to light it, but his expression remained shuttered, and she was not sure what to believe. 'I still don't understand why you thought it necessary to make such a suggestion.'

'I had my reasons, and I don't wish to discuss them at the moment,' he said sternly, his teeth clenched about the stem of his pipe and smoke billowing from his mouth as he dropped the burnt-out match into an ashtray.

'But surely I'm——' Entitled to an explanation, she had wanted to say, but she was not given the opportunity.

'*Enough!*' he barked, smoke jetting from his nostrils when he removed the pipe from his mouth, and Jo paled visibly at the dark fury she glimpsed in his eyes. 'This subject is no longer open for discussion, Joceline! Do I make myself *clear*?'

'Absolutely.'

Jo was feeling faint. The floor seemed to be moving beneath her feet, but she somehow managed to remain standing until Rafe had stalked out of the living-room. Only then did she sink into the nearest armchair, and all thought of Averil Andersen was now swept from her mind.

The dizziness passed swiftly, but Jo remained seated a moment longer with her hand resting lightly against her flat stomach. She could no longer ignore what was happening to her. The natural cycle of her body had been disrupted, and during the past weeks the sudden dizzy spells and telling bouts of nausea had become a regular occurrence.

She was pregnant. Jo was now almost convinced of this, but it would be wiser to keep this knowledge to herself until she could have it confirmed.

Averil looked rested when she joined them for dinner that evening. She was polite enough not to ignore Jo, but whatever she said seemed to be directed mainly at Rafe. Jo did not resent being left out of the conversation since it gave her the opportunity to study them more closely, but observing them together brought her no nearer to the truth. Rafe held himself aloof from his mother while Averil treated her son with a great deal of wariness and, studying them unobtrusively while she ate, Jo wished she knew the reason for this unhappy situation.

Their coffee was served to them in the living-room, and shortly after nine that evening, before retiring, Averil went to her flat and emerged moments later with a large, square box which had been wrapped in silver and blue striped paper.

'I bought something for you as a wedding present in Waterford, Ireland,' she said, placing the package on the low marble-topped table.

The clock on the mantelshelf ticked away the seconds, but Rafe made no move towards the gift his mother had presented to them, and Jo shifted her position nervously to the edge of her chair. 'Shall I open it?' she asked, feeling awkward as she glanced up at the older woman, who had remained standing.

Averil nodded, her autocratic features giving away none of her feelings, and Jo despised herself for the tremor in her hands as she carefully unwrapped the gift.

A salad bowl of the finest crystal emerged from among the protective mound of tissue paper, and Jo drew an audible breath of delight as she took it out of the box. She lifted it out for Rafe to see and, caught in the firelight, a myriad colours emerged in little sparks from the intricately carved crystal. It was one of the most beautiful things Jo had ever seen, and she stared at it in speechless fascination.

'It was kind of you to think of us, Mother,' Rafe announced from the depths of his armchair, his voice impersonal as if he were talking to a stranger, and Jo felt like taking him and shaking him when she glimpsed that look of pain and disappointment in his mother's eyes.

She placed the bowl on the table and rose quickly to kiss the older woman on the cheek. 'Thank you very much for this beautiful gift, Mrs Andersen.'

'I'm glad you like it,' Averil responded tonelessly, her eyes devoid of the smile which curved her mouth. 'Goodnight.'

Jo swallowed at the lump in her throat and blinked back her tears as the inter-leading door closed behind Averil, but she was shocked and angry the next instant when she turned towards Rafe to see him lounging in his chair as if he didn't have a care in the world.

How *could* he? she wondered furiously. How could he sit there and not be touched by his mother's unhappiness?

'I don't know what could have happened to make you change so monstrously, but I do believe that the gentle, caring man I used to know must still be lurking there somewhere deep inside you.' Her eyes flashed green fire at him. 'I suggest you find that man, Rafe, and find him *soon*!'

She stormed out of the living-room in a fury, her footsteps echoing sharply across the tiled hall before they became muted in the carpeted passage. Rafe made no attempt to follow her, and that was a blessing. She was perilously close to bursting into tears, but she was damned if she was going to break down emotionally in front of him.

Jo was lost in thought the following afternoon when she sat on the stoep, and she was only vaguely aware of Elsie emerging from the house with a tray of tea, which she placed on the cane table.

She had seen Averil briefly at teatime that morning, but it was at the luncheon table that she had seen Rafe for the first time that day, and then his silent, sombre mood had not encouraged conversation. He had left the dining-room as soon as he had finished eating to closet himself in his study, and Averil had followed suit to retire to her flat.

Left to her own devices again, and too restless to lie down, Jo had taken her crochet work out on to the shady stoep, but her thoughts, rather than the crochet hook, had done most of the work.

It had been so hot all day that it felt like summer rather than the first day of spring, and Jo was fanning herself with the crochet pattern leaflet when the sound of an approaching car shattered the Sunday afternoon silence.

It was Lorin's white BMW that churned up the dust in the driveway to come to a crunching halt beneath the shady elm, and Jo felt that old familiar tension gripping her insides. Lorin and Averil had once been allies, ganging up to make her life a misery, but they were not going to be allowed to do it again.

Jo rose from her chair and forced a welcoming smile to her lips as Lorin started to ascend the steps on to the stoep. 'Good afternoon, Lorin.'

'I'm not here to see you,' Lorin announced rudely as she breezed past Jo towards the entrance of the house.

'*Lorin!*' That icy note of authority in Jo's voice had stopped many a bigoted intern in his tracks, and Lorin reacted to it in much the same way. She stopped and turned towards Jo with a startled look on her face. 'I didn't think for one moment that you had come here to see me,' Jo informed her coldly, 'but this *is* my home, and you could at least be civil.'

Lorin was quick to pull herself out of that brief moment of stunned surprise. 'This could never be your home, because you don't belong here, and you never will.'

You don't belong! That old refrain evoked painful memories of the past, but Jo had to think of the future, and the future of the child she believed she might be carrying.

'You've got that wrong, Lorin,' she corrected with an icy calm. '*You're* the one who doesn't belong here, and, unless you acquire a few manners, I will not have you in my house or anywhere around it.'

'You can't speak to me like that!' Lorin exclaimed haughtily. 'Who the hell do you think you are?'

'She's my wife!' Rafe's voice reached them from the opposite end of the stoep, and Jo heard the rasping intake of Lorin's breath as they swung round simultaneously to see him walking towards them with a thunderous expression on his face. 'Jo is my wife,' he repeated in a voice that had an ominous ring to it, 'and I echo every word she said, Lorin. If you can't be civil to her, most especially in her own home, then you're not welcome here.'

His supportive statement sent a glowing warmth surging through Jo, but it had an adverse effect on Lorin. Her face went a sickly, pasty colour, and there was pure venom in those brilliant blue eyes that met Jo's briefly before she turned without speaking and strode out to where she had parked her car.

Jo placed her hand lightly on Rafe's arm, gaining his attention when Lorin sped down the driveway in her BMW, and the tension inside her did not diminish when she felt the quivering tautness of the muscles beneath the hair-roughened warmth of his skin. 'Thank you for supporting me, Rafe.'

His dark gaze seemed to soften, and he started to say something, but Averil chose that moment to join them on the stoep.

'Didn't I hear Lorin's voice out here a few moments ago?' she asked, glancing about her curiously.

'You did, Mother,' Rafe confirmed as they stepped towards the cane table and chairs where the tray of tea awaited them.

'Why didn't she stay and have tea with us?' Averil wanted to know, her questioning glance demanding an explanation from Jo, but it was Rafe who answered her.

'I told Lorin that she wouldn't be welcome here in future if she couldn't be civil to my wife.'

'Oh.'

Averil had breathed the word almost cautiously into the explosive little silence which had followed Rafe's statement, and Jo wondered at the thoughts behind the shuttered expression which had shifted across her mother-in-law's face.

'May I pour your tea, Mrs Andersen?' Jo asked with a calmness she was far from experiencing at that moment as she reached for the teapot.

'Yes, please,' Averil replied in that subdued fashion which Jo still found so difficult to accept.

The Averil Andersen of three years ago would never have yielded so readily to her son, Jo was thinking as they sat drinking their tea. It had been Rafe who had done most of the yielding, allowing his mother to have her way with almost everything desired, but now the situation was quite the reverse.

The questions flitting through Jo's mind were becoming repetitive, like a hi-fi needle caught in the groove of a faulty record, and she knew she had to shut the questions off or go quietly mad with not knowing.

CHAPTER EIGHT

IT WAS not until the Wednesday of the following week that Jo had the opportunity to consult a doctor, whose name she had chosen at random in the Beaufort West telephone directory. He could neither reject nor confirm her suspicion that she was pregnant, but he did promise that she would have the results of the tests that same day.

A hot breeze churned up the dust in the parched veld, and driving back from town that morning Jo had seen the clouds gathering on the western horizon. The clouds had been heavy with the promise of rain, but she already knew how easily they could fade into nothing when they reached the arid plains of the Karoo.

They needed rain. Jo had reached this conclusion long before Rafe had mentioned it at the breakfast table that morning. Everyone was praying for one good downpour, and after that they would go on praying, for nothing was feared more in the Karoo than the long summer months without rain.

Jo was alone in the house after lunch that afternoon when she received the call she had been waiting for. The tests had been positive. She was pregnant with the child Rafe had demanded in exchange for the loan.

She felt like crying as she lowered herself shakily on to the straight-backed chair beside the telephone table in the hall. She had not misread the signs of pregnancy, but having her suspicions confirmed had come as a shock.

No, it wasn't shock that was making her want to weep. What she felt at that moment was *fear*. How would Rafe react to the news that she was going to have his child? If all went well he would have his heir before the winter of the following year. What then? Would she be reduced to an unwanted thorn in Rafe's side once she had fulfilled her side of this hateful bargain?

No! The word rose like an anguished cry from her soul and echoed through her mind like a wailing siren. Please, God . . . no, she shot up the silent but fervent prayer.

Jo was in complete control of herself again when, later that afternoon, she joined her mother-in-law for tea in the living-room. She had poured their tea and was offering Averil one of her favourite ginger biscuits when she heard the thundering hoofs of a hard-driven horse approaching the house.

'Something's wrong,' Averil voiced Jo's thoughts, and not two minutes later Elsie was hovering anxiously in the living-room doorway.

'It's Stan, madam,' she said, her explanation directed at Jo. 'He says Klara has gone into labour, and the midwife is sick in bed with bronchitis. Stan isn't sure if there's still enough time to get Klara to the hospital, and he wants to know if you could come and help.'

Jo placed her untouched cup of tea on the tray and said calmly, 'Tell Stan I'll be at his house as soon as I can, and he should go home and stay with his wife.'

Elsie left at a running pace to pass on that message while Jo excused herself from Averil to collect her medical bag which she had stowed away at the bottom of her dressing-room cupboard.

On her way out she thought it best to leave a message for Rafe with his mother, and she changed her direction to make a hasty detour past the living-room. 'If I'm not back before dinner, Mrs Andersen, would you please explain the situation to Rafe?'

'Of course.' Averil's glance stated clearly that she was weighing Jo mentally and finding her wanting. 'I think it would be unwise of you to meddle with something you know nothing about, and I suggest you convince Stan that the hospital would be the best place for his wife.'

Jo felt her hackles rise. Stay calm, she warned herself. 'I did midwifery as part of my training, Mrs Andersen, and you may rest assured that I'll know what's best for Klara after I've examined her.'

She spun on her heel and left, not caring at that moment if her reply had annoyed her mother-in-law. She had more important things to worry about, she was thinking as she drove away from the house, and the weather was one of them, she realised as she cast a frowning glance up at the sky.

The clouds had accumulated during the course of the day and it looked as if there was a storm on the way. She could see lightning flashes in the distance, and the first heavy drops of rain splashed on to the Jetta's windscreen when she neared Stan's cottage, where his horse was still tethered to the fence.

An unexpected crack of thunder shook the earth as Jo got out of her car to make a dash for the entrance of the cottage, and she could not help feeling sorry for the tethered animal when she saw it flick back its ears and paw the ground nervously.

She banged on the cottage door before opening it and stepping inside to escape the violence of the approaching storm, and she was walking down the passage, past a smartly furnished lounge, when Klara's stifled moans guided her in the direction of the bedroom.

Klara was lying on the bed, her olive-skinned features registering pain and glistening with perspiration. Stan was seated on a chair beside the bed, but he jumped up the moment he saw Jo, his expression fluctuating between relief and anxiety.

'Thank you for coming, madam,' said Klara, smiling up at Jo despite the pain of her contraction, and Jo took her hand between her own and squeezed it reassuringly.

'I'd like to examine your wife, Stan, so why don't you go out and stable your horse before the storm really hits us?'

Stan nodded and got up to leave, but at the door he paused to cast an anxious glance at his wife. 'I won't be long,' he promised, and then he left.

'I don't want to go to the hospital,' Klara stated worriedly the moment they were alone. 'If you would help me, madam, then I want this baby to be born here at home.'

'If the birth is progressing normally, then I see no reason why your baby shouldn't be born here at home.' Jo placed her bag on the chair Stan had vacated and opened it to take out the items she required. 'Now, let's take a look at you, Klara.'

Wind-driven rain lashed the bedroom window and the foundations of the cottage seemed to shudder with every vicious clap of thunder while Jo carried out her examination. The storm was almost directly overhead when a disturbing thought crossed her mind. Would the road be passable after this deluge? She wondered about this for a moment, but then a more important issue took precedence in her mind.

'It feels like a big baby, Klara,' she finally voiced her opinion above the noise of the storm. 'The heartbeat is strong, and since everything appears to be progressing normally I see no reason for your baby not to be born here at home, but it's still going to take a while.'

Klara looked relieved and a dreamy look entered her dark brown eyes. 'I don't want to have more children after this, so I'm hoping for a boy.'

'I can imagine that after having three girls you and Stan must be very anxious to have a boy.' Jo smiled at Klara while she straightened the sheets. 'Talking about the girls, where are they?'

'Elsie's daughter, Violet, is looking after them until this is all over. They're going to sleep at her place tonight and—*oh*!'

The explanation ended on a groan and Jo slid her hand beneath the sheet to place it against the woman's hard, distended abdomen.

'Just try to relax, Klara,' she instructed calmly. 'Breathe deeply through your nose. That's it. Now blow the air out slowly and strongly through your mouth.'

Klara followed Jo's instructions implicitly, breathing deeply and exhaling through her mouth several times until the contraction eased.

A door slammed somewhere to the back of the house and moments later Stan was entering the bedroom. 'How is she?' he demanded anxiously of Jo.

'The baby won't be born for a couple of hours yet, but your wife is going to be fine.'

'Stop worrying about me, Stan,' Klara rebuked her husband gently.

'Were you present at the birth of your daughters, Stan?' Jo asked when he seated himself on the bed beside Klara, and he shook his head ruefully.

'The midwife always said this was no place for a man and that I should wait outside until it was all over.'

'Would you like to stay this time?'

Stan cast a questioning glance at Klara, then he looked up at Jo and nodded affirmatively. 'Thank you, madam, I'd like to stay.'

Klara's baby was born at fifteen minutes past seven that evening as the storm reached a peak of violence that had the foundations of the cottage shuddering beneath their feet, but Stan had remained beside his wife to hold her hand and to encourage her with loving words throughout the painful trauma of birth.

'It's a boy!' he shouted excitedly when, with a little encouragement from Jo, the infant gave its first cry. 'It's a boy, Klara!'

'Praise be to God!' was all Klara said, and there were tears of joy in her eyes when she held out her arms to receive her baby.

At that moment Jo could not help thinking about the new life growing in her own womb, and she felt deeply emotional as she laid the baby in Klara's arms. This was not the first time in her life she had witnessed the miracle of birth, but never before had it touched her quite so profoundly.

It was still raining steadily at eight-thirty that evening when Jo picked up her bag and leaned over the cradle. She was smiling as she brushed the tip of her finger lightly across the sleeping baby's soft, warm cheek, but her smile faded when she straightened to cast a clinical glance at the mother. Klara lay in bed, propped up against the pillows. She looked exhausted, but exhaustion had failed to dim that glow of pride and happiness on her face.

'I suggest you do what your son is doing, Klara,' Jo advised sternly. 'Get some rest.'

'I'll sleep now,' Klara promised, reaching out for Jo's hand and clasping it tightly. 'God bless you for being here to help, madam.'

'I'll come again in the morning, but don't hesitate to call me in the night if you should need me.'

Klara nodded, and Jo took one last look at the sleeping child before she turned towards the door where Stan stood waiting with an umbrella to escort her out to her car.

'Drive carefully, Madam Jo,' he warned when she left the shelter of the umbrella to slide behind the wheel of her Jetta. 'The road is going to be muddy and slippery in this rain.'

'I'll be careful,' she promised. 'Goodnight, Stan.'

It was a dark night. Lightning forked intermittently across the sky in the distance, but it was still raining so heavily that the windscreen wipers had difficulty trying to cope with the deluge of water. Visibility was bad, and Jo drove slowly on the slippery farm track, but she picked up speed eventually when she felt the Jetta hold the road firmly despite the fact that the wheels spun occasionally in the muddy earth.

The road curved sharply up ahead, then dipped steeply and rose again. She was halfway home, Jo was thinking with a measure of relief while she negotiated the bend and steered the car down into the dip, but the next instant her heart leapt anxiously into her throat. The car was sliding sideways and the wheels were spinning dangerously in the mud. She changed down to a lower gear and by some miracle managed to keep the car going until she could feel the tyres gripping firmer ground.

'Thank God!' she breathed on a sigh of relief, but she did not relax behind the wheel again until she saw the lights of the house up ahead through the trees.

She garaged her car and made a dash for the house. The distance from the garages to the kitchen door was no more than twenty metres, but her sleeveless cotton frock offered no protection against the rain that pelted her from all sides, and she was soaked to the skin long before she reached the cover of the back stoep.

The door was flung open before Jo could reach it, and Rafe was silhouetted darkly and dangerously against the kitchen light. The grimness of his expression deepened during the ensuing seconds, and she realised suddenly what a sight she must look. Her hair had fallen free of the combs to hang in wet tendrils about her face and shoulders, her dress was clinging to her body like a second skin, and the water draining off her was collecting swiftly in a puddle beneath her sandalled feet.

'For God's sake, come inside,' he ordered, drawing her shivering form into the kitchen and shutting the door against the stormy elements outside. 'Is everything all right?'

That was an all-encompassing query, and it was so typical of Rafe that Jo could not suppress a snort of laughter. 'Everything's fine with mother and child. And I'm fine too, except that I'm drenched and frozen.'

'You'd better get out of those wet clothes at once and into a hot bath,' he advised sternly.

Jo could not fault that advice. There was nothing she needed more at that moment than to immerse herself in a hot bath. Her teeth had started to chatter, she was getting so cold, and she almost ran the distance from the kitchen to their bedroom.

Half an hour later, relaxed and warm after a steaming bath, she had wrapped herself up in her quilted dressing-gown and she was sitting cross-legged on the bed while she towelled her hair dry. The storm had passed, but she could still hear the rain pelting the window-panes when the bedroom door opened and she looked up through an untidy veil of damp hair to see Rafe walking towards her with a mug in his hand.

'Feeling better?' he asked, seating himself on the edge of the bed and turning so that he was facing her.

'Much better, thank you.'

Her heart was beating a fraction harder and faster against her ribs as she discarded her towel and pulled her brush through her damp, stringy hair in an attempt to restore some order to her appearance. Was the dimness of the bedside light to blame for that extraordinary softening of his ruggedly handsome features?

A mug appeared in her line of vision. 'I made you some cocoa,' he said.

'Thank you.'

She put down the brush to take the mug from him, and their fingers touched. He did not remove his hand at once and, when he did, a current of awareness was surging through her that made her throat feel oddly tight as she raised the mug to her lips to sip at the hot cocoa he had prepared for her.

'You must be tired,' he remarked.

'At the moment I'm still too keyed up to feel tired.' Her eyes met Rafe's over the rim of the mug and she smiled as she recalled the excitement and happiness she had witnessed earlier that evening. 'Stan and Klara have a son.'

An answering smile touched his strong yet sensuously chiselled mouth, and the smile deepened until it creased the corners of his eyes. 'They were hoping for a boy.'

'So Klara told me.'

And you, Rafe? Jo questioned him silently. Would you want a boy? Or would you be happy with a girl?

She lowered her lashes hastily in fear of what he might see in her eyes. He had a right to know that he was going to be a father, but she was not yet ready to tell him.

'I'll get you something to eat,' he said into the silence when she was swallowing down the last mouthful of cocoa.

'No, please don't.' Her fingers caught at his arm, detaining him when he would have got up to leave. 'I had a mug of soup and a sandwich with Stan and Klara before I came home, and I'm really not hungry.'

She was hungry for conversation, not food. If Rafe left now, then her mental buoyancy would turn to frustration. There was so much inside her that cried to come out, so much that needed to be shared, and she did not wait for an invitation from Rafe to lapse into a résumé of everything that had occurred during those long hours she had spent at Klara's bedside.

Rafe asked questions and listened intently when she answered him in a voice that was lowered and calm despite that detectable undertone of excitement. His eyes lingered on her face while she spoke, and at times his features actually softened into a bone-melting smile that awakened memories of the past.

This was the old Rafe, Jo was thinking when her voice finally trailed off into silence. This was the Rafe she had always found it so easy to talk to; this was the gentle, caring man she had fallen so madly in love with all those years ago, and her soul reached out in recognition and longing.

Tell me I'm not mistaken, Rafe. Touch me and show me you still care.

'You always give unstintingly of yourself to others,' he said softly, his fiery eyes responding to her silent plea and touching her in a way that made her body feel heated and eager beneath the quilted dressing-gown. 'Do you have anything left of yourself to give to me?'

'I'm giving of myself now, aren't I?' The emotional tension between them was becoming un-bearably laced with desire, but something told Jo that she would have to make the first move. She folded her legs in beneath her and, without breaking eye contact, took off her dressing-gown. 'Make love to me, Rafe. Please?'

'You don't have to beg,' he said, framing her face with his hands and smiling as he leaned forward to take her lips and everything else she was offering him.

Jo opened her mouth to his, inviting the intoxi-cating invasion of his tongue while her body wel-comed the exciting touch of his hands. She tried to control the stabbing urgency of her emotions when Rafe cupped her breasts in his palms, but her control snapped when his thumbs moved back and forth across their rosy peaks in an electrifying caress, and she moaned her pleasure into his mouth.

Her fingers fumbled with his shirt buttons, and if Rafe had not helped her she might have ripped the expensive cotton in her eagerness to touch him without the annoying barrier of his clothes. She wanted him as she had never wanted him before, her body was beginning to ache with the intensity of her need, and when she had freed him of his shirt she unashamedly trailed a path of heated kisses from the hollow of his throat down across his hair-roughened chest until the explorative tip of her tongue encountered a hardened male nipple.

Rafe groaned and, encouraged by the knowledge that she was pleasing him, she ventured on, but his fingers bit into her waist, and she was lifted higher on to her knees until her breasts were on a level with his face. His flicking tongue teased her nipples into swollen nodules throbbing with a need he had not yet satisfied. She locked her fingers into the hair at the back of his head in an attempt to draw him closer, but still he held back.

'Please, Rafe! You know what I want! Please!' she begged huskily, her body straining towards that tantalising tongue.

Only then did he relent, but, even so, it was Jo who leaned into that warm, moist mouth which had been tormenting her and driving her mad with desire.

A shuddering moan escaped her as he sucked gently first at one nipple and then the other, arousing a longing so intense that her body arched against his. The pleasurable torment continued as he eased her over on to her back to trail his mouth and hands lightly and sensually over every centimetre of her heated body right down to the sensitive soles of her feet.

Jo felt drugged with desire, and she was scarcely aware of breathing when Rafe parted her legs to trail a path of fiery kisses along the softness of her inner thighs, but when he reached the core of her womanhood she cried out in the wake of her body's flaring response to this unfamiliar caress.

'No, Rafe! *Don't!*'

That pleading voice seemed far removed from her own as she struggled to free herself from the rasping intimacy of his tongue, but his weight on the lower half of her body held her a prisoner. And then it was too late. Her body spasmed on a strange surge of pleasure, and then stilled beneath him.

'Oh, God!' She raised her forearm over her face to hide her shame and embarrassment. 'I'm sorry. You—you shouldn't have done that.'

'I had to.' He rubbed his stubbly chin against her hip-bone. 'You were much too impatient.'

'But now it's over.'

'It isn't over yet, Jo,' he promised. 'Not for me, and most certainly not for you.'

She watched him with heavy-lidded eyes as he got up to take off the rest of his clothes, and she marvelled as always at the magnificence of his body when he leaned over her with his muscles taut like those of a predatory animal preparing to vanquish its prey.

'You're crazy!' she gasped in protest when he lowered his naked body on to hers and sought her mouth with his own. 'I can't...I couldn't possibly...'

But she did!

Rafe aroused her skilfully, taking her once again to that frantic peak of desire where her mind clouded over to let her body take charge of its own search for satisfaction.

I love you. The words hovered on the perimeter of Jo's conscious mind, but they remained unspoken as their heated bodies melded in the rhythmic harmony of shared passion. I love you, Rafe. She wanted him to know this, and the only way she could tell him was to give herself to him— body and soul—for the first time since entering into this unpalatable marriage.

Jo awoke early the following morning, but not early enough to speak to Rafe before he left the house. Last night, when they drifted off to sleep, she had wanted to tell him that she was going to have his baby, but in the end she had remained silent for fear of shattering that feeling of contentment she had known in the aftermath of their lovemaking.

She would tell him later when they met for breakfast, she was thinking as she got up and dressed herself to go out, and she could only pray that her earlier fears would not be realised. After last night—after what she believed they had shared—he wouldn't reject her. Would he?

The sun had just risen when Jo drove out to Stan's cottage. The storm had wreaked havoc with the farm road, but the earth seemed to rejoice in its wetness, and Jo knew that soon a multitude of indigenous, succulent plants would emerge from the hidden recesses of the dry soil to cover the scrub-covered land with a carpet of colourful flowers.

Klara had risen and was taking care of herself and the baby when Jo arrived at the cottage. Stan had gone to fetch the girls, and Jo did not stay longer than the few minutes it took to examine the mother and her baby.

Later that morning, when she faced Rafe across the breakfast table, she changed her mind about divulging her secret. The gentle, caring Rafe of the night before was gone, and in his place was the harsh-faced stranger she had married two months ago. Jo had believed that last night would mark a turning-point in her marriage to Rafe, but she had been sadly mistaken.

'You didn't have a decent meal last night, and you're not eating your breakfast this morning.'

Rafe's accusing statement made her focus her glance on the fried egg which was beginning to congeal on her plate, and her face paled. A wave of nausea rose inside her, and beads of perspiration were breaking out on her forehead when she got up and fled.

She somehow reached the bathroom in time to accommodate her convulsing stomach, and she slumped over the basin as she felt herself being turned inside out. She retched violently, again and again, but the only thing she succeeded in doing was to exhaust herself. When the nausea finally passed she sat down weakly on the edge of the bath with tears in her eyes, and that was when she realised that she was no longer alone.

Rafe was there, and he was holding a glass of water to her lips. She gulped down a mouthful to ease that burning sensation at the back of her throat, and then he was carrying her into the bedroom as if she weighed no more than a child.

He lowered her gently on to the bed and sat down beside her, his features grim in the morning light that filtered into the room through the lacy curtains at the window. 'I take it you're pregnant.'

That cold, cryptic statement unleashed the pain and anger she had locked away inside her for so long. 'Yes, *damn you,* I'm *pregnant*!'

The words had come out in a furious hiss through her teeth, and then, to her horror, she burst into tears. She rolled away from him to bury her face in her pillow, but Rafe pulled her up into his arms and held her with her face buried against the hollow of his shoulder.

'For God's sake, don't cry.' He stroked her hair with gentle fingers and rocked her in his arms as one might rock a child in distress. 'Please, Jo, I can't bear to see you crying.'

'I always w-wanted to—to have your child,' she wept brokenly into his khaki-clad shoulder. 'But n-not like this. Not in—in exchange for a—a l-loan. It's so——'

'There was no loan.'

'—barbaric and—and so utterly immoral. I don't think I—— ' Jo's voice hiccuped into silence as his words, spoken over hers, suddenly penetrated. They made no sense, but they had a sobering effect, and she drew a shuddering breath as she tilted her head back to stare up at him through the film of tears in her eyes. 'What did you say?' she demanded shakily, convinced that she must have heard him incorrectly.

Rafe held her probing glance for a moment, then he released her and got to his feet. 'I said there *was* no loan,' he repeated grimly.

'I—I don't understand,' she murmured, brushing the tears out of her eyes with the back of her hand, and trying to make sense out of the confusion inside her while she watched him sweep the lace curtains aside at the window as if he suddenly had a desperate need for more air.

'I wanted you back. It's as simple as that,' he explained harshly. 'I knew you wouldn't return to Satanslaagte of your own free will, and I suspected that if I asked you to marry me again you'd turn me down flat, so between Danny and myself we devised the story about the loan.'

Jo stared at that broad, formidable back which was turned so resolutely towards her. Has he gone mad, or have I? she wondered.

'Why did you want me back?' she demanded, ignoring the latter half of his statement for the moment.

'Why?' The hand clutching the lace curtain closed into a fist that made the muscles in his tanned forearm bunch together. 'Because I should never have let you go in the first place,' he announced with an unexpected savagery.

Jo's mind was reeling drunkenly between the shocking truth and disbelief. Suddenly nothing made sense to her, and she wondered if anything ever would again.

She swung her feet down to the carpeted floor and rose slowly. There was a fierce clamouring inside her, like a volcano threatening to erupt, but there was one question that still needed an answer. 'If Danny's need for a loan was a farce, then I presume your desperate need for an heir was also a fabrication?'

'It was the only way I could think of to coerce you into a normal marriage.'

'How could you *do* this to me?' Humiliation and anger flared hotly in her cheeks, but the ice of winter was in her voice. 'How *could* you?'

He turned then, and there was an odd whiteness about his mouth when he came towards her. 'Jo, I know how——'

'Don't touch me! Don't even come near me!' Her eyes sparked green fury as she shrank beyond the reach of the hands he held out to her. 'I think you're contemptible!'

CHAPTER NINE

'I THINK you're contemptible!'

Jo's words were still hanging uncontested in the air between Rafe and herself when a sharp knock on the bedroom door shattered the angry silence, and her fury was still seeking an outlet when she flung open the door to find an anxious-looking Elsie hovering on the threshold.

'I'm sorry, madam, but Madam Averil is not well and she's asking for you.'

Averil's pride would not have allowed her to send for Jo unless it was a matter of some urgency, and it was this knowledge that penetrated the mists of Jo's anger to make her shelve her personal problems for the moment. She stormed down the L-shaped passage ahead of Rafe, and she was almost running when she crossed the lounge to enter the flat through the inter-leading door.

Jo found Averil lying in bed, her silvery hair in disarray, and her hands clutching agitatedly at the bedclothes which she had pulled up to beneath her chin when they entered her bedroom without knocking. Her breathing was audibly fast and laboured, she was feverish to the touch, and in between racking coughs she complained of a pain in her back.

Jo suspected bronchitis, and her fingers were resting firmly against Averil's wrist, checking her pulse-rate, when she realised that Rafe was observing her silently and intently from the opposite side of the bed.

'I suggest you get in touch with your doctor,' she said, giving him no more than a cursory glance.

Averil gestured protestingly, but Rafe took no notice. He left the room and when he returned a few minutes later he was looking pale and grim. 'Dr Bosman is already out on a call, but his wife promised to get in touch with him, and he'll be here as soon as he can make it.'

Jo made Averil as comfortable as she could, and almost an hour passed before they heard a car approaching the house. Rafe got up to investigate, and when he returned a few minutes later he was not alone. An elderly man, carrying a medical bag, preceded Rafe into the bedroom, and the look of almost smiling recognition on Averil's face made Jo conclude that this man had been doctor and family friend for many years. Rafe performed the necessary introduction, then left the room so that the medical practitioner could carry out his examination.

'It's acute bronchitis,' the doctor finally confirmed Jo's suspicions. 'A few days in bed with the proper care and medication will soon clear it up.'

'I can't stay in bed,' Averil protested in between rasping coughs.

'You can and you *will* stay in bed, Averil,' the doctor instructed sternly while he put away his stethoscope and closed his bag. 'If you don't do as you're told the bronchitis could develop into something which would force me to hospitalise you, and you know how you hate hospitals.'

Averil's fit of coughing subsided and she glowered up at the doctor even while she sagged exhaustedly against the pillows. 'You're just trying to frighten me into complying with your wishes.'

'You know me too well to believe I'd do something like that, Averil.' Dr Bosman eyed his patient speculatively for several moments. 'I think it might be a good idea if I sent someone along from the hospital to nurse you through the next few days.'

Averil's feverish glance shifted to Jo with just a hint of a plea in those dark eyes. 'That won't be necessary, Dr Bosman,' Jo intervened calmly in response to that surprising plea. 'I'm a qualified nurse, and I'm quite prepared to see to it that Mrs Andersen gets all the rest and care she might need through the next few days.'

The doctor nodded his approval and, after exchanging a few words with Rafe in the lounge, he left.

Jo seldom left Averil's bedside during the next three days and nights, and the only time she saw Rafe was when he came in briefly to check on his mother's progress.

Those long hours of nursing Averil through the fever and bouts of coughing had left Jo with little time to think about herself. It was during the fourth night, when Averil slept peacefully for the first time, that Jo's thoughts drifted back for the first time to that morning when Rafe had told her that Danny's financial plight had been part of a diabolical plot to force her into a situation she had not sought.

She had been tricked into marrying Rafe again. Her brother—and possibly also her mother—had guided her skilfully towards that meeting with Rafe in Beaufort West's Mirage Hôtel, and she had walked with her eyes wide open into their well-laid trap.

Jo wished she could hate Rafe, but what she felt for him was not hate. She loved him, and that unalterable fact was something she had learned to live with a long time ago. She had been hurt and incredibly angry on discovering the truth, but at that moment she was calm and rational, and she was not consciously groping for understanding when fragments of Rafe's statements started to flit through her mind.

'I wanted you back'…'It's as simple as that'…'I knew you wouldn't return to Satanslaagte of your own free will'…'I should never have let you go in the first place.'

The thoughts came and went until she sat up in her chair with a jolt, her mind suddenly alerted to something she had missed before. She could remember asking Rafe why he had wanted her back, and his answer had been, 'Because I should never have let you go in the first place.'

Her heart was behaving like a wild thing in her breast, almost choking off the air from her lungs. Could she interpret that to mean that Rafe had wanted her back because, like herself, he had never stopped caring? Jo wished she could believe that, she so desperately wanted it to be true, but there were still so many pieces missing to this puzzle that she dared not allow herself to hope too much.

'Why don't you get some rest, Jo? I'm feeling so much better.'

Jo looked up sharply at the sound of that wavering voice, and she leapt self-consciously to her feet beside the bed in the dimly lit room. 'I didn't realise you were awake, Mrs Andersen.'

'I've been lying awake for quite some time,' Averil said, staring up at Jo with an unfathomable expression in those dark eyes which constantly reminded Jo of Rafe.

'Could I get you something to drink? A glass of warm milk, perhaps?'

Averil shook her silvery head against the pillows. 'Just a mouthful of water would do, thank you.'

Jo poured some water into a glass and slid her arm beneath Averil's shoulders to raise her. She held the glass to Averil's lips, and Averil drank from it until she indicated with a slight wave of her hand that she had had enough. Jo lowered her on to the pillows again and disposed of the glass, but she felt a little uneasy when she realised that those dark eyes had been following every movement she had made.

'Please sit down, Jo.' Averil shifted her legs to make room for Jo on the side of the bed, and Jo seated herself warily. 'You've been very good to me, and God knows I've done nothing to deserve your kindness.'

Jo felt awkward. She could sense that Averil had something on her mind; she could even guess at what it might be, and suddenly she could not bear the thought of this proud woman having to humble herself. 'Mrs Andersen, there's no need for you to—— '

'Don't interrupt me, Jo,' Averil cut across her words. 'No matter what I do I can't escape the fact that I've been a foolish old woman. I owe you an apology, but more than that I owe you an expla-

nation, and I can only pray that there may come a
time when you'll find it in your heart to forgive
me.'

Jo sat stiffly and silently on the edge of the bed
with her hands clasped together so tightly in her
lap that her fingers went numb. She wished she
could call a halt to this conversation, but she
somehow knew that Averil would not rest until she
had emptied herself of everything that troubled her.
Perhaps that was for the best, but for Jo there was
no joy in this thought.

'I felt threatened by your presence the first time
you married Rafe, and I was jealous of the love my
son had for you.' Averil's confession contained a
simple honesty which Jo found touching. 'Everything I said and did during that time stemmed from
those two cancerous emotions, and I admit that I
also used Lorin shamelessly to further my cause.'

Jo had been aware of the latter, and she had also
known that Lorin's obvious infatuation for Rafe
had led her into becoming a very willing participant.

'I wanted to drive you away from Rafe and away
from Satanslaagte,' Averil continued, her voice
growing stronger in her determination not to spare
herself. 'I succeeded on both counts, but in the
process I also succeeded in driving my son away
from me, and I deserved his wrath when he discovered the part I'd played in ruining your marriage. Rafe had been terribly unhappy after you left,
but when he knew the truth he became almost demented, and I didn't doubt that he'd be moving
heaven and earth to get you back.' Tears glinted in
Averil's eyes, but she was smiling as she lay there
looking up at Jo. 'I want you to know, and to be-

lieve, that I'm glad he was successful in persuading you to marry him again.'

Jo's gaze was thoughtful as she watched her mother-in-law dab at the moisture in her eyes with a clean handkerchief. It took courage to openly admit one's mistakes, and at that moment Jo could not help but admire this woman who had once caused her so much pain.

'Why did you agree to Rafe's suggestion that you move into this flat?' she asked, steering the conversation towards a subject which had troubled her for some weeks.

'It's been proved that it could be disastrous to have two women in one household.' Averil laughed softly for the first time as she slipped her handkerchief into the cuff of her bedjacket, but her features sobered the next instant, and a faintly embarrassed expression flitted across her face. 'It didn't work for me with my mother-in-law all those years ago when I came to Satanslaagte as a bride, and we both know that it didn't work for *you* with *me.*'

Jo felt compassionate tears pricking at her eyelids. 'You were always a vital part of this household, and for me you always will be.' Her voice dipped almost to a whisper as she added, 'You're going to be needed now more than ever before.'

'What do you mean?' Averil demanded, subjecting Jo to the intense scrutiny of her dark eyes. 'In what way could I possibly be needed?'

'You're going to become a grandmother in the not too distant future, and a child needs its grandparents as much as it needs its mother and father.'

Averil stared up at Jo in startled, contemplative silence, then those autocratic features softened in a way that brought an aching lump to Jo's throat. 'Oh, my dear, what can I say?'

Jo took one of Averil's heavily veined hands between her own and clasped it firmly. 'Just tell me that you're happy for Rafe and for me... Mother.'

This was the first time she had dared to call Averil Andersen 'Mother', and Averil's eyes were shimmering with tears again as she curled her fingers about Jo's in a gesture of acknowledgement. 'I can tell you how happy I really am for Rafe and for you... my *daughter*.'

It seemed like a miracle. That gaping chasm between them had at last been bridged, and Jo sat there on the side of the bed for a long time, holding Averil's hand contentedly without either of them feeling the need to speak. She was reluctant to break the companionable silence between them, but she knew she had to when her glance finally shifted to the clock on the bedside cupboard.

'It's eleven-thirty,' she said, getting up reluctantly to straighten the bedclothes. 'We still have a long night ahead of us, and I really think you should try to go to sleep again.'

'I don't think I'm going to be able to sleep,' Averil protested with a joyful smile. 'I'm so happy we've had this talk, and I'm too excited at the prospect of becoming a grandmother!'

Despite Averil's protestations she was asleep half an hour later, and only then did Jo make herself comfortable on the couch which had been her bed for the past three nights. She was tired and in desperate need of a few hours' undisturbed sleep, but her mind remained annoyingly active.

Where was Rafe? Was he asleep, or was he lying awake and thinking of her as she was thinking of him at that moment? Did he still care? Was that why he had been so underhandedly determined to get her back? Averil had said, 'I was jealous of the love my son had for you,' but Jo could not help thinking that "had" was the operative word in that statement. If Rafe still loved her, then why didn't he tell her so? Why was he still hiding his feelings beneath that savage exterior which had frightened her into submission on so many occasions during these past months?

A helpless, despairing sigh escaped her as she turned her cheek into the pillow and tried to go to sleep. There were still so many questions racing through her mind, and they were all crying out to be answered. It made her head spin just to think of it, but the questions would have to wait until she had the opportunity to resume that hateful and humiliating conversation with Rafe which Elsie had interrupted several days ago.

Averil was well enough the following morning to sit up in a chair, and Jo left her there in Elsie's care while she went to her own room to shower and change into fresh clothes. Jo had hoped to see Rafe before he left the house that morning, but she was still trying to do something with her hair before going to breakfast when she saw him drive off in the truck.

She did not expect to see Rafe during the course of that morning, but when he didn't come home for lunch she started to worry. She was being silly, she told herself, but that afternoon, as she was collecting Averil's tray of tea in the kitchen, she found herself voicing her feelings to Elsie.

'I'm a bit worried, Elsie,' she said. 'Why hasn't Master Rafe been home today?'

'Master Rafe hasn't been home much these past few days, madam, and he said this morning that we mustn't expect him home until late this evening.' Elsie put down the knife she had been using to peel the potatoes and turned to stare out of the window while she wiped her hands on a kitchen towel. 'They're putting up new fences where the old ones had been washed away in the last storm, and if you ask me, madam, there's another storm brewing.'

Jo followed the direction of Elsie's gaze and understood what she meant about 'another storm brewing'. Dark clouds were gathering in the distance, and they were rolling ominously across the arid plains. If the wind did not change, then the Karoo veld could expect to receive yet another lashing of rain before evening.

The heat was oppressive and full of promise, but the storm never materialised during that afternoon. The clouds simply disintegrated over the heated basin between the flat-topped hills, and those that survived the distance were blown away when the wind veered unexpectedly in a different direction.

Rafe came home earlier than expected that evening. Jo saw him for the first time in the dining-room after he had showered and changed into brown trousers and a white, short-sleeved shirt and, looking at him properly for the first time in days, she was shocked to see the exhaustion etched so deeply into his tanned features.

'How's Mother?' he asked when they seated themselves at the dinner table to share a meal for the first time since Averil had been taken ill.

'Your mother was well enough to get up out of bed today and she enjoyed sitting in a chair for short spells.'

Rafe accepted this information with a brief inclination of his head, but Jo had the strangest feeling that the query had been delivered automatically, and that he had not heard one word of her response to it. His face wore a grim mask and his manner was coldly withdrawn. It made any attempt at conversation impossible while they ate their meal, and Jo was actually relieved when Rafe finally left the table with the muttered excuse that he had work to do in his study.

'I haven't seen Rafe today,' Averil complained when Jo went in to see her. 'Hasn't he come home yet?'

'He came in late, and when he left the dinner table he went straight into his study.'

A look of disappointment flashed across Averil's face, and it tugged sharply at Jo's heart. She would have to talk to Rafe about this chilling relationship between himself and his mother, and the sooner she did so the better for all of them.

There was no need that night for Jo to continue her vigil at Averil's bedside. She could sleep in a comfortable bed again, and she was looking forward to this when she went into the kitchen shortly before ten that evening to make herself a mug of cocoa before retiring. She took a mug out of the cupboard and then, on an impulse, took out a second mug and added milk to the amount she had already poured into the saucepan on the stove.

This was *crazy*! She was bound to have her head bitten off for intruding where she was not wanted, she was thinking minutes later as she placed the mugs on a tray and carried it through to the study. There was a nervous fluttering at the pit of her stomach when she paused outside the door, but she raised her hand determinedly and rapped on the panelled wood.

She knocked a second time, and still she received no response from within the study. Was Rafe deliberately ignoring her request to enter, or was he so involved in what he was doing that he'd simply not heard her knock? Jo could feel her courage threatening to desert her, but she had not come this far only to turn back, and it was with that thought in mind that she opened the door quietly and went inside.

The stench of stale tobacco was the first thing that hit her when she entered the book-lined study, but what she saw was enough to make her heart miss several anxious, thudding beats. Rafe lay slumped across his cluttered desk with his head resting on his forearms. His favourite pipe lay beside an over-full ashtray, and close at hand was an empty bottle of whisky beside an overturned glass. Rafe seldom had a drink. Why would he suddenly want to drink himself into a stupor?

Jo shifted a pile of papers on the desk to make room for the tray and opened the window to let in some air before she placed a tentative hand on Rafe's shoulder. He stirred the instant she touched him, and she withdrew her hand hastily when he sat up abruptly to focus his sleep-laden eyes on her.

'What do you want?' he demanded, looking vulnerable and oddly on the defensive as he sagged back into his chair.

'I thought you might like a mug of cocoa.' Jo shifted her glance meaningfully towards the empty bottle of whisky and overturned glass. 'Perhaps a cup of strong black coffee would be more appropriate.'

His smile was twisted as he righted the glass, and his features looked haggard beyond the pool of light which the reading lamp spilled across his desk. 'The bottle contained no more than a double tot of whisky, so a mug of cocoa will do fine.'

Jo knew a certain amount of relief, but nervousness and uncertainty were still gripping her insides as she passed him his mug of cocoa and seated herself to face him across the width of the teak desk.

The silence between them was strained, and then the echoes of their last verbal altercation rose between them to hover there like an awkward but challenging barrier. It was Rafe who had made the first shattering move towards total honesty between them that morning when he had learned that she was going to have his child. It was up to her now to make the next move. Jo sensed it, and she knew with every fibre of her being that she dared not let this moment pass.

'I know you're tired, Rafe,' she began tentatively, 'but we have to talk.'

His eyes flickered strangely and he reached for his pipe, but he changed his mind and combed his fingers through his hair instead in a totally uncharacteristic gesture. 'You were right, you know. What I did was utterly contemptible.'

'Perhaps not quite so contemptible if the entire truth were known,' she countered gravely. 'I'm convinced there's more to what you told me the other day, and I think you owe me a more detailed explanation.'

Rafe reached for his pipe again, and this time he did not change his mind. He clenched the stem between his teeth, struck a match, and cupped his hand about the flame. He took his time lighting his pipe, then rose slowly behind his desk to stand with his back to her in front of the open window. The pleasant aroma of pipe tobacco was carried towards her on the cool night breeze, and she was beginning to think she would never know the truth when Rafe lapsed into the explanation she had been waiting for.

'What I have to tell you is a long saga of misguided conceptions which resulted from a break in communication, and my own lack of perceptiveness.' He spoke without turning, but Jo detected a note of bitterness in that deep, gravelly voice. 'When I married you the first time I just took it for granted that you'd be happy here at Satanslaagte, but you weren't, and knowing this just tore me apart inside until I began to feel like a selfish lout for taking my happiness at your expense.'

Jo felt the pain of the past wash over her with all its ferocity, and she cringed inwardly. Misguided conceptions? A break in communication? That was what had eventually driven them apart, and ... dear God ... she was as much to blame for that as Rafe, she confessed to herself as she waited for him to continue.

'I found myself believing that our marriage had been a mistake, and that you would have been happier if I'd left you in your natural environment, but the *biggest* mistake I made was to ask you for a divorce.' He turned slowly and frowned down at the pipe in his hand as if he was wondering how it had got there. 'I realised my error soon after you left. My life without you had become aimless, but unfortunately it was too late to do anything about it.'

Jo folded her hands together in her lap to still their trembling. 'You could have stopped the divorce proceedings.'

'Yes, I could have stopped the divorce proceedings, but stubborn pride prevented me from doing so.' He smiled, but his smile was tainted with bitterness and anger as he leaned back against the window-sill and crossed one long leg over the other. 'I'd made a hash of things, Jo, and I was too damn proud to crawl back and admit that I'd been wrong.'

Jo could understand and accept that statement as she sat pale and still in her chair. 'What happened then?' she prompted quietly.

'Last year in April, on my thirty-sixth birthday, to be exact, my mother and I were having dinner that evening when your name suddenly entered into the conversation, and that was when Mother inadvertently let something slip. I realised then that she'd been largely to blame for your unhappiness and discontent, and we ended up having a flaming row.' His stabbing gaze met hers, and the accusation in the dark depths of his eyes made her stir uncomfortably in her chair. 'Why didn't you tell me what was going on, Jo? Why did you leave me in ignorance?'

It was Jo's turn to explain, and it took courage to sustain his probing glance while she delved back mentally into the past to recount the circumstances which had caused that final rift between them.

'I didn't want to cause friction between you and your mother,' she confessed in a voice that was not as steady as she would have wished it to be. 'You're your mother's only child, and I believed that with time and patience the problem would eventually resolve itself, but I was wrong. It got worse instead of better. When I wanted to confide in you I found that you'd drifted so far away from me that you'd become an unapproachable stranger. And then I simply lost heart.'

Her voice broke on that last sentence. It hurt to talk about that time, but she had to, and she willed herself to continue.

'I began to believe that the things your mother had said were true. Life in the city hadn't prepared me for the unfamiliar rigours of life on a sheep farm, and I didn't belong. I also agreed that Lorin, with her knowledge of the land, would have been a much better wife to you.'

Rafe was silent for what seemed like an eternity while he assimilated everything she had told him. A tiny vein was pulsing against his temple, and then he was gesturing angrily with the hand that held the pipe. 'I have never—*never*, understand?—had the slightest desire to marry Lorin. She grew up before my eyes, and even though you're both about the same age I've never thought of her as anything other than an amusing child who also happened to have a good knowledge of farming.'

'I believe you.' There had never been any real doubt in Jo's mind that Rafe's feelings for Lorin had been purely platonic, but it was balm to her battered soul to hear him say it. 'What happened after you had that row with your mother?' she asked, steering the conversation back on to a more important track.

'I left here in a rage the following morning and drove down to Cape Town.' He walked towards her and seated himself on the corner of the desk close to her chair. 'I wanted to see you again, to explain, and I was determined that I'd succeed in persuading you to return to Satanslaagte with me.'

So Rafe had gone to Cape Town during that week away from the farm, Jo was thinking as she recalled the information Elsie had passed on to her. 'I was never aware of the fact that you'd been in Cape Town, so I can only assume that something must have happened to make you change your mind about contacting me.'

'I visited your home, but you were doing a stint of night duty at the hospital, so I spent an enlightening evening with your mother and Danny.' He disposed of his pipe and combed his fingers through his hair again so that it fell untidily across his broad forehead, and accentuated the haggard look on his face. 'I told them everything, and we talked for a long time, but in the end they didn't hold out much hope for me where you were concerned. They said you'd been adamant about never wanting to see or hear from me again, and that you'd forbidden the use of my name in your presence.' His tired eyes burned into hers for a moment, then he sighed audibly and looked away. 'I knew then exactly how much I'd hurt you, and in those circumstances I felt I didn't have the right to force my way back into your life.'

Rafe was sitting so close to her that she barely had to lift her hand to be able to touch his hard thigh, and she wanted to, but ... not yet. There was still too much that had to be said between them.

'But you *did* eventually force your way back into my life,' she responded with a forced calmness to his statement.

'Yes, I did.' His expression had darkened, and he got up to stand in front of the window again with his hands thrust deep into the pockets of his trousers. 'Danny phoned me unexpectedly about a month before we were married, and he told me something to make me believe that you might still care.'

Jo stared at those broad shoulders, and they suddenly seemed to be sagging with something more than just ordinary fatigue. 'If you believed that I might still care, then why didn't you approach me in the usual way instead of inventing that monstrous lie to force me back into your life?'

'Danny told me something else as well.' He turned abruptly and pinned her to the chair with those dark, piercing eyes. 'He said you'd sworn never to set foot on Andersen soil again even if I should come to you on bended knees. Do you remember?'

So *that* was it!

'Yes, I remember.' How could she forget her reply to Danny's query whether she would marry Rafe again if he should ask her? Jo lowered her glance guiltily, but then her latent anger flared up again. She leapt to her feet and crossed the room to lean with her hands against the ornately carved top of the oak cabinet, but in her present state of mind she was blind to the academic trophies behind the glass doors. *'Damn!'* she muttered furiously to herself rather than to Rafe. 'What a fool I was not to have seen through it all, but Danny was so confoundedly convincing when he pleaded with me to approach you for a loan to save the company.'

'My success depended on Danny's acting abilities, and he told me afterwards that he sweated like a pig at the thought that he might say or do something to make you suspect the truth.'

The nightmare of the past few months was beginning to evolve into something a great deal more palatable, but Jo was not yet ready to forgive anyone, least of all her brother for his treacherous behaviour. He had known her loyalty was of such a nature that she would do almost anything to prevent them from losing the company and their home, and she had fallen for his ruse like a novice.

CHAPTER TEN

A COOL breeze drifted into the study through the open window, bringing with it the sweet scent of gardenias and the sound of the insects chirping in the undergrowth. A jackal howled in the distance and from somewhere in the garden the Alsatian responded with a warning bark. It disturbed the tranquillity of the night outside, but neither was there anything tranquil about the way Jo was feeling at that moment as she let her hands fall away from the trophy cabinet.

She was simmering inside with an anger which was directed solely at herself. If she had sorted out the problem years ago between Averil and herself, then none of this would have happened. She would have felt safe and secure in her marriage instead of having to wonder if her husband still loved her, or whether he had wanted her back purely for the sake of revenge.

She turned slowly. Rafe was still standing at the window, watching her with shuttered eyes and waiting. Waiting for what? she wondered uneasily.

'Did my mother know?' she asked, breaking the strained silence between them.

Rafe shook his head. 'Danny and I decided it might be safer not to let her in on the secret until after you and I were married.'

This explained why her mother had not answered her letters during those first weeks after their marriage. It also explained why her mother had sounded anxious and decidedly odd on the telephone. Lavinia Harris would have put a stop to Rafe's and Danny's plans had she known, and Jo could imagine that her mother must have felt guilty about the part she had inadvertently played in this deception.

A wave of overwhelming tiredness washed through her mind and over her body. It drove her towards the chair she had vacated, and she sat down heavily. 'Why did you do it, Rafe?' she asked.

She was tired of this uncertainty and of having to feed her hungry heart on the crumbs of supposition. It was time she knew the truth, and was told exactly where she stood, she was thinking while she tried to probe beneath the surface of that grim mask Rafe was wearing.

'Why did you force me into this marriage under such hateful circumstances?' she asked, rephrasing her query when he remained silent.

Rafe still appeared in no hurry to answer her. His chin had sagged down on to his chest, and the thumb and forefinger of one hand were pressed against his closed eyelids as if to ease a burning behind them, then his hand fell limply to his side.

'Two years of misery and regret can eat away at a man's soul,' he said, the rawness of emotion adding a biting harshness to his low, throaty voice. 'But I believe the final destruction was caused by the disillusionment and anger I've had to live with since discovering my mother's treachery.'

Jo waited in silence for him to continue, but there was something indefinable in his dark, compelling gaze that made her hopeful heart quicken its pace.

'I was in a fury because of what my mother had done, and I was angry knowing that you allowed our marriage to be destroyed by not confiding in me, but most of all I was furious with myself for having been so blind to the things which had happened right under my very nose.' His smile was twisted with self-derision as he pushed himself away from the window to seat himself on the corner of the desk nearest to Jo. 'I wanted you back, and I think I became more than just a little deranged in my determination to succeed.'

'So you got me back. Between you and my brother I was cleverly tricked into marrying you again, but it still wasn't enough for you, was it?' Jo was at last beginning to understand, and with understanding there came a curious sense of release. 'I had to be punished for the part I played in causing your misery. You wanted to see me hurting as you had hurt, and if you could cause me pain and mental anguish, then it would ease some of the pain and anguish you've had to endure. That was what you thought, wasn't it?'

'Yes.' His mouth tightened. 'Dastardly as it may seem, that's how I felt about it.'

'You succeeded very well in your objective, but...' she drew a painful breath '...didn't it ever occur to you that I might have suffered as well?'

'The thought did cross my mind, but when one is hurting badly one tends to think selfishly only of oneself.' He reached out as if he wished to stroke some colour into her pale cheeks with his fingers, but he halted the action and withdrew his hand with a touching uncertainty. 'I had so much anger buried deep down inside me. It was like a volcano that threatened periodically to erupt, and there was nothing I could do to stop it,' he went on, remorse deepening the grooves that tiredness had already etched on his ruggedly handsome features. 'I'm aware that I behaved like a savage beast at times and, if it's of any consolation to you, I've done nothing but despise myself these past months for the way I've been treating you.'

Jo knew an intense desire to reach out and touch him. She wanted to comfort him and be comforted in return, but her own uncertainty held her immobile in the chair. 'When were you actually planning on telling me the truth?' she queried.

'I'm not sure.' He moved his shoulders beneath his tailored shirt as if the cotton had suddenly shrunk to cause an uncomfortable tautness across his broad back. 'There were so many times when I came close to confessing everything, to explaining that the loan was a hoax, but something always held me back—my confounded pride again, I guess— and afterwards I would hate myself for being such a damned coward.'

'I don't believe you're a coward.'

'Don't you? Well, I call it cowardly when I think of how I shied away from telling you the truth because I feared the contempt I felt so certain you would have for me, but the other morning, when I realised you were pregnant, I no longer had a choice. I'd never seen you cry so bitterly before, and it just cut me up inside. I knew then that I couldn't leave it there. I had to tell you the truth even though the timing was rotten.' Rafe leaned towards her, and her sensitive nostrils quivered with the not unpleasant mixture of masculine cologne and pipe tobacco which clung to his clothes, but her mind was registering an unfamiliar look of anxiety in his eyes. 'Where do we go from here, Jo?'

Jo stared up at him solemnly. Where did they go from here? She was not sure. Everything Rafe had said seemed to suggest that he still cared, and she had no doubt at all about her own feelings, but she was still too wary to bare her soul to him.

She looked away as her thoughts shifted to Averil Andersen, and she found herself recalling with clarity that look of disappointment she had seen on the older woman's face earlier that evening. Averil had paid dearly for her mistakes, just as they had all paid for their mistakes in one way or the other over the years, but Jo knew she could never make a serious bid for her own happiness while knowing she was the cause of the ill feeling that still existed between Rafe and his mother.

'Your mother and I had a long and revealing talk last night,' she told him. 'Or perhaps I should say that your mother did most of the talking and I listened.'

She glimpsed a tiny nerve pulsing in Rafe's jaw in response to her statement. This was a touchy subject, and she knew he might not approve of her interference, but she had to go on.

'We've made our peace, Rafe. There are no longer any feelings of animosity between us, but now it's your turn to go and make your peace with her. Your mother regrets her actions of the past, and even more so because it's driven this wedge between you. She loves you, Rafe. You're her only child. Can't you find it in your heart to forgive her?'

The tautness about his stern mouth relaxed a fraction. 'It still hurts when I think of what she did to me, but she *is* my mother, and I've naturally forgiven her a long time ago.'

'Your mother isn't aware of this, and how will she know it if you don't tell her?'

'Very well, you've made your point. I'll go in and see her first thing in the morning,' he promised gravely, but then he brushed the matter aside with an impatient and rather imperious wave of his hand. 'I want to know about *us*, Jo,' he demanded with an urgency which was laced with that unfamiliar anxiety she had noticed earlier. 'You'd better accept the fact that I'm never going to let you go again, so where do we go from here?'

'We've both made so many mistakes in the past,' she replied, her voice unsteady as that flame of hope inside her was suddenly kindled into a roaring fire. 'Let's not make any more if we can help it.'

'Tell me, Jo... and I want the truth.' He leaned towards her, his compelling glance holding hers and stabbing relentlessly at those barriers which she was still too wary to dismantle entirely. 'If I'd come to you during those weeks before our divorce was finalised... would you have given our marriage a second chance?'

Jo considered this seriously for a moment, then she shook her head. 'Probably not,' she answered him with a faintly cynical smile curving her soft mouth. 'I would have said that you didn't know your own mind, that your feelings for me were inconsistent and not to be trusted, and I would have been too afraid to take a chance on being hurt again.'

His eyelids flickered briefly as if she had touched him on the raw. 'What about last year in April, Jo? What if I'd come to you then? Would you have given me an earful and sent me packing, or would you have allowed me to talk to you—to explain?'

'I don't know. I'm not sure what I would have done.' Her features settled into a thoughtful repose, but her glance did not waver from his while she tried to answer him truthfully. 'So much has happened in between *then* and *now*. You forced me to marry you, I've been sharing your bed again for almost two and a half months, and now I'm in the initial stages of pregnancy. In the present circumstances I find it difficult to imagine how I might have reacted more than a year ago, but that's not important any more. Is it?'

'No, that isn't important any more.' The grooves running from his nose to his mouth had deepened, making him look gaunt and much older than his thirty-six years. 'I've been a real brute to you, Jo. Have I made you hate me very much?'

She was not deaf to the underlying urgency in that casual query, but she could not stop herself from smiling a little wryly. 'If my brother was acting as your spy, and I think I have every reason to believe that he was, then there ought to be no need for me to answer that question.'

'I never asked Danny to spy on you, but, when I asked him, he told me that he believed your feelings for me hadn't altered, and it was on the strength of that assumption that I based my actions.'

Jo was still digesting this information when his hands reached out, and their rough warmth enveloped hers in an almost punishing grip.

'Physically we still knock sparks off each other, but I want much more than that from you, Jo,' he continued with some urgency. 'I want the entire packaging, and I want to be a part of every little thing that goes into making up the whole. So, if Danny's information was correct—and I'm still not absolutely convinced that it was—would you consider this new deal I'm offering you?'

'If this is a roundabout way of asking me whether I still care, then the answer is "yes".' There was no sense in continuing to hide what lay in her heart, and she lifted the veil on her heart's secret as her clear green gaze held his. 'No matter what's gone before, and no matter what may happen in the future, my feelings for you will always remain the same. I love you, Rafe.'

'Thank God for that!'

He was on his feet in one lithe movement, the tension and anxiety easing out of his face, but relief did not lend itself to gentleness when he pulled her up out of the chair and into his arms.

Jo was shaking, but so was Rafe. She could feel the tremors racking his body while they stood locked in that fierce embrace. There was no need to speak, it was as if their minds had suddenly switched into the same wavelength, and several soul-restoring moments elapsed before Rafe relaxed the crushing pressure of his arms around her to prise her face out into the open with strong but gentle fingers.

'I love you, Jo.' There was a tender warmth in the eyes that traced every rise and hollow of her delicate features, and her heart filled with a joy so intense that it brought a lump to her throat. 'I love you,' he said again as if to make sure she had heard him.

'You've never said that to me before,' she whispered, her voice choked with emotion and her eyes filling with tears of happiness.

'What haven't I said before, my darling?' he demanded softly against her quivering mouth.

'That you love me.'

'Didn't I?' His head went up, and his expression registered a certain incredulity, but the burning intensity of his eyes had long ago told her much more than words ever could. 'Didn't I ever tell you that I love you?'

She shook her head at him, and smiled tremulously through her tears as she leaned back against the circle of his arms. 'No, you didn't. You said, "I want you," plenty of times, but you never said, "I love you."'

Rafe considered this gravely for a moment, and then, surprisingly, a rueful look flitted across his face. 'I guess I've always had this tendency to be more explicit about the unimportant issues, but words always seem to fail me when I have to discuss the things I care most about.' He drew her close again and gently kissed away the tears that glistened on her lashes. 'Do you think you could ever forgive me for making such a hash of our lives and for being such a cad to you these past months?'

'I think I might,' she teased, 'but it's bound to be a long process which may take years, and until then, I'm afraid, you're stuck with me.'

'Take your time, my love. Take your time,' he said, laughing softly down into green eyes that sparkled with mischief. 'I can't think of anything I'd like more than being stuck with you for the rest of my life.'

'You must be a glutton for punishment, my darling husband,' she teased.

'Punishment can always be made tolerable by spicing it with the occasional dash of pleasure.'

There was a deliberate sensuality in his lowered voice, and Jo's senses were leaping wildly in response when he picked her up in his arms and carried her through the silent house to their bedroom.

Later that night, when they lay awake but wonderfully content in each other's arms, Rafe shifted his position slightly and laid his hand gently against Jo's lower abdomen, which still gave no outward indication of her pregnancy.

'About the baby——' he began, his eyes darkening with concern, but Jo silenced him with her fingers against his lips.

'I want this baby, Rafe, and I'm very happy about it.' There was a tender warmth in her voice and in her touch as she combed her fingers through his hair and tugged playfully at the greying strands against his temples. 'I know now that this child was conceived in love and not really by demand, and that makes all the difference.'

'I want this baby too, and not for the callous reason I mentioned before. Please believe that, Jo.'

'I believe you.' Her fingers lovingly explored the hollows and planes of his features, and she looked up at him with eyes that glowed with the feelings she no longer needed to hide. 'I'm glad you've banished the devil I was forced to marry under such hateful circumstances, and I would like to welcome back the man I married for the first time four years ago. That's the man I never will stop loving.'

'God knows, I love you, Jo,' Rafe groaned, capturing her hand in his and kissing the soft tip of each finger in turn. 'I may not always say it, but I want you always to know it and to feel it.'

'I know it now, and I feel it. And I'll never doubt it again,' she promised against his descending mouth as she curled herself into his body and surrendered herself once again to the pleasure of his skilful manipulations.

It was odd, but when she finally drifted off to sleep that night she was aware of a new sense of belonging. For the first time she could think of Satanslaagte and acknowledge that this was *home*.

She belonged . . . at last.

MY VALENTINE 1992

Celebrate the most romantic day of the year with
MY VALENTINE 1992—a sexy new collection of four
romantic stories written by our famous Temptation
authors:

> GINA WILKINS
> KRISTINE ROLOFSON
> JOANN ROSS
> VICKI LEWIS THOMPSON

My Valentine 1992—an exquisite escape into a romantic
and sensuous world.

 Harlequin Books

VAL-92-R

HARLEQUIN
PROUDLY PRESENTS
A DAZZLING NEW CONCEPT IN ROMANCE FICTION

One small town—twelve terrific love stories

Welcome to Tyler, Wisconsin—a town full of people
you'll enjoy getting to know, memorable friends and
unforgettable lovers, and a long-buried secret that
lurks beneath its serene surface....

JOIN US FOR A YEAR IN THE LIFE OF TYLER

Each book set in Tyler is a self-contained love story;
together, the twelve novels stitch the fabric of a
community.

LOSE YOUR HEART TO TYLER!

The excitement begins in March 1992, with
WHIRLWIND, by Nancy Martin. When lively, brash
Liza Baron arrives home unexpectedly, she moves
into the old family lodge, where the silent and
mysterious Cliff Forrester has been living in seclusion
for years....

WATCH FOR ALL TWELVE BOOKS
OF THE TYLER SERIES
Available wherever Harlequin books are sold

Janet Dailey
Americana

A romantic tour of America through fifty favorite
Harlequin Presents novels, each one set in a different
state, and researched by Janet and her husband, Bill.
A journey of a lifetime in one cherished collection.

Don't miss the romantic stories set in these states:

Available wherever
Harlequin books are sold.

JD-MAR